God bless you!

Pamela Barber

THE INSIDER

PAMELA BARBER

WESTBOW°
PRESS
A DIVISION OF THOMAS NELSON
& ZONDERVAN

WestBow Press books may be ordered through booksellers or by contacting:

WestBow Press
A Division of Thomas Nelson & Zondervan
1663 Liberty Drive
Bloomington, IN 47403
www.westbowpress.com
1 (866) 928-1240

ISBN: 978-1-4908-5391-8 (sc)
ISBN: 978-1-4908-5390-1 (hc)
ISBN: 978-1-4908-5392-5 (e)

Library of Congress Control Number: 2014917379

Printed in the United States of America.

WestBow Press rev. date: 10/31/2014

CONTENTS

Chapter 1   The Door 1
Chapter 2   The Sin in Josh's Heart 9
Chapter 3   The Study Room 13
Chapter 4   The Kitchen and Dining Room 18
Chapter 5   The Living Room... 29
Chapter 6   The Work Shop.. 35
Chapter 7   The Rec Room.. 41
Chapter 8   The Bedroom 49
Chapter 9   The Bathroom.. 59
Chapter 10   The Medicine Chest...67
Chapter 11   The Armor Closet...75
Chapter 12   The Storage Closet...84
Chapter 13   The Treasure Room..96
Chapter 14   The Car and the Garage 105
Chapter 15   The Front Yard.. 116
Chapter 16   The Fruit Tree 127
Chapter 17   The Fishing Boat... 137
Chapter 18   The Sidewalk... 148
Chapter 19   The Angel on the Roof... 159
Chapter 20   The Word Hidden in his Heart 172

1

—∞∞∞—

The Door

"Goodnight Joe." said Joshua to the owner of the restaurant where he worked part time. "Have a good one, Josh! Oh, and take that bag of garbage to the dumpster on your way out, thanks Josh!" Joe called out. Joe was a pretty good boss, not that Joshua has had a lot of them to compare him to. But he's fair and notices Josh's hard work. As Joshua hurls the big bag of garbage over the edge of the dumpster, it catches on something and rips open. "Oh come on, you can't be serious!" The nasty mess from the bag fell everywhere, including on his new shoes. "Great, just what I needed!" he muttered to himself.

As he walked back to get something to clean up with, he thought of the lecture his mom would dish out once he got home. Her talks usually started out fine, but they seem to always end up being about everything she thinks he isn't doing right with his life. How he wished he had enough money to move to a place of his own so he didn't have to listen to it all the time. He had just turned nineteen. He was out of high school and he was trying to figure out what he wanted to do with his life. Maybe he lacked ambition or maybe he was just confused. Anyway, he needed more time to think. He was interested in a lot of different things but he just couldn't decide what direction to go. Should he go to college, the navy, or just wait here until he knew for sure?

"Back so soon?" Joe asked when he saw Josh come in. "I thought you were going home?" "The garbage bag ripped open and there's a huge mess out there!" Josh explained. Joe could tell Josh was upset, when he saw his shoes, he knew why. "I just bought these shoes! Fifty bucks wasted!" Josh said angrily. "I'm sorry that happened to you Josh, I know how hard you work for your money. I'm sure you can clean them up as good as new." Joe said as he grabbed a broom and a new bag. "Nah, they're ruined. I'll just throw them out." Josh complained. He always tried to keep his belongings in pristine condition and hated it when things got spotted or damaged. "Well, that's too bad. I'll go clean up outside while you wipe them off." Joe said.

"Thanks Joe, I'll be right out." Joshua was a lot calmer as he walked outside to help Joe. "I'm sure you'd rather be doing anything other than cleaning this mess up." Josh said as he held the dust pan. "Oh it's alright, I don't mind, It's all part of the job." Joe said. "I don't know how you stay so cool all the time Joe. I mean, you don't seem to get mad about anything." Joshua said. "Oh believe me, I do. I just have an inner super power that helps me to stay calm when I feel like I'm gonna lose it." Joe said.

"Is that right? Is it like Superman or something?" Josh laughed. "Hmm, Superman, that would be interesting. No my inner power comes from God." Joe said as he finished putting the garbage in the bag. "If you say so, whatever it is it definitely works for you." Josh said. "You know Josh, God doesn't throw us out when we are messed up. He can clean us up better than new, if we ask him to." Josh didn't respond but it got him thinking about God.

He rolled down the window to enjoy the warm spring night as he drove home. Angel Cross was a mid-size town with a small town feel to it. It was pretty quiet most nights, aside from a party or two on the weekends. There was hardly any crime to speak of. Overall, it was a pretty nice place to live. There was large lake with a sandy beach on the one side of town, which was a big attraction for tourists. A lighthouse and a beautiful boat harbor made it look more like New England than the mid-west. There were a couple of new hotels and a variety of shops and eateries along the walkway. The town itself was nestled between some large rolling hills, which made it look even more picturesque. Josh lived in the middle of the historic part town with his mom and sister. His brother had joined the navy, had his training and was already at sea, his dad went to work in another part of the world and hadn't been seen or heard from in two years.

Josh thought about how much he had learned from Joe since he'd been working for him. Joe seemed to always be saying something wise. He didn't push his religion on anyone, but everyone knew he was a Christian just by the way he acted and the way he treated others. *"Joe is a good man, and I really respect that in him,"* Joshua thought to himself. So he made a promise to himself to get to know Joe better and try to be more like him. *"So what if dad gets jealous of me spending time with Joe,"* Josh thought. *"After all, he's the one who left us! Ah, he can just stay there for all I care!"* Thinking about his dad put him back in a bad mood. To top it off, the lid came off of his drink when he lifted it out of the cup holder and it spilled all over the seat cushions and floor mat. "That's perfect, now my seats are ruined too!" He yelled.

Josh didn't yet realize that his anger was flowing out of the resentment he had for his parents. His dad was working in some distant place on some sort of "top secret project" or so his mom had told him. Derek specialized in repairing oil drilling machinery. Josh was really having a hard time believing that a project could take two years to complete and in all that time his dad hadn't called home once. He was beginning to believe that his dad had abandoned his family for someone else. Josh felt rejected, and for over a year it had become his responsibility to watch over his younger sister Bethany since his mom went to work full time. Bethany wasn't a little kid, but she needed someone to be there at night with her. He was mad that his mom had gotten a job that kept her away so much, especially since his dad was sending checks to support them. Then there was Caleb, his older brother. Before he went into the navy, Caleb would take off with his friends almost every night and leave Josh alone to supervise Bethany. Josh knew Caleb was going to drinking parties, but he never said anything to his mom about it. What really made him mad was how Caleb was always put on a pedestal by his mom. She seemed to believe he was always so good. And now to make matters worse, his sister Bethany was acting strange, she was always so outgoing before, now she was always in her room on her laptop. It's like she was trying to isolate herself from everyone. It was really upsetting to him and he was worried about her. He blamed his parents for that too. The worst part was that Bethany used to tell him everything, now she barely spoke to him. He was feeling alone and empty inside and he needed something or someone to fill the void.

He huffed as he slammed the car door shut and then did the same to the back door as he came into the house. His mother had just gotten home and was about to start a three week vacation. "Josh, is that you?" she called out from the other room. "I don't want to hear it!" he yelled back. "I was just going to tell you that there's some leftover chicken and potatoes in the fridge, and why are you in such a bad mood?" She asked. "Will you stop, you're always getting on me about something!" he snapped. "No I'm not, you're exaggerating!" She said as she walked into the kitchen. "The bible says you should honor your parents!" She added "Oh, stop with the God stuff mom. You and dad are not perfect parents, you know!" he said sarcastically. "I never said we were Josh, but we try! I love you, but lately, your attitude towards me is so bad and disrespectful that I don't even recognize you anymore." She said, almost in tears. "Why are you so angry with me? You don't talk to other people like that! I just don't understand it Josh!" She said emotionally. "I'm not in the mood to talk, I'm going to bed!" He said as he stomped up the stairs. All of the resentment, rejection and frustration he felt came out in angry outbursts that he couldn't control.

As he sat on the edge of his bed in the dark, he began to feel guilty for the way he had talked to his mom. *"I don't know why I get so mad at her, she isn't that bad." He thought.* Josh really did love his mom, so why couldn't he get past these feelings? *"What's wrong with me? God help me, I'm so sorry for acting like a jerk to my mom. Are you real God? Can you hear me? I feel so alone, and I don't understand why I'm even here. What's the meaning of life anyway?"* He talked silently to the ceiling, hoping someone up there had heard him and would answer back. He kicked his shoes off and put his head back on his pillow. He was too tired to get undressed and within minutes, he was sleeping.

Josh felt the curtain blow gently across his face. *"What a nice cool breeze,"* he thought. He sat up and stretched. *"Where am I? Whose house am I in?* He thought as he stood up and looked around. The place seemed familiar, and yet he knew he'd never been there before. As he walked from room to room, he couldn't help but think that it was decorated with the exact things he would use if he had his own place. It was so weird to feel like you belonged in a place where you'd never been before, but that's how it felt, like it was his place. Suddenly he heard a knock at the door. Not knowing whose house he was in, he wasn't sure what he should do. Whoever it was kept knocking, so Josh peeked out the window to see if he could get a look at the person. He could only see the man from the side, so he couldn't tell who it was.

"Hello. Is there something I can help you with?" asked Josh. The long haired man with a beard smiled and said, "I was going to ask you that." "I don't understand, why would you come here to help me?" asked Josh. "I came because you asked me to." The man replied. "I think you have the wrong house mister. I mean, you do seem familiar to me, but I don't think I know you." "Well, you have me there. You don't know me, but I know you, in fact, I've known you all your life!" The man said. Josh was confused. *"How is that possible?"* he thought. "Because I created you!" the man explained. Josh slammed the door before he even realized he'd done it. *"Am I losing it? Oh man, I'm going to be committed to one of those places for people who hear voices in their* heads!" he thought. A light knock on the door brought him back from that awful thought.

He slowly opened the door enough to see the man. "Okay, so what did I ask you to help me with?" The man didn't act upset about having a door slammed in his face. "I get the feeling that you need my help with quite a lot, Joshua," the man said, in a friendly voice. *"He knows my name!"* Josh thought. "I told you, I know you, so of course I know your name. I created you!" For some reason, Josh was less freaked out this time when the man somehow heard his thoughts. He decided to go with it, asking him questions he thought he would never know the answers to. But he did know. He knew everything about Josh's life, even the secret thoughts he had. "I never asked you for your name," Josh said. "My name is Yeshua or Jesus in English" the man answered. "Is it really you?" Joshua asked with excitement. "You heard my prayer, I can't believe it!" "May I come in Joshua?" Jesus asked. "I don't know who lives here," Joshua answered.

"I have news for you Joshua, this is your house! It's actually your heart. If you invite me to come in, I will dwell here with you. I'll comfort you and guide you, I'll help you with everything! Please let me come in Joshua, I love you, I always have," Jesus said as he gently touched his hand. Peace and joy flooded into Josh's heart, like liquid love flowing from God himself into every part of his being. Josh fell to his knees. Being in the presence of such holiness and love made him realize just how sinful and lost he really was. "Will you forgive me Lord? I know in my heart that I have sinned. I need you to help me and save me! Please come into my heart Jesus!" Joshua said as he opened the door all the way. Jesus helped him to his feet. "That's why I came here tonight." Jesus hugged Josh then he walked into the house, kicked off his sandals, hung up his robe and said, "It's good to be home!"

2

⊶∞∞⊷

The Sin in Josh's Heart

As Jesus walked with him through the house, Josh became deeply embarrassed and ashamed of the way things looked. "Sorry my house is so trashed Lord." "Don't you worry about it I'll take care of this stuff." Jesus said as he rolled up his sleeves. "Just take a seat over there." He pointed to a chair where Josh could sit and watch. "Can I help you?" Josh asked. "No, I'm the only one who can clean hearts. When I died on the cross, the blood I shed and the suffering I endured, paid for all your sin, past, present and future. All you have to do is believe it and trust in me. It's my gift to you, so just receive it." Jesus took a key from his pocket, bent down by Josh's feet and unlocked the shackles and chains that had been around his ankles. As they fell away, Josh gasped, "I didn't know I was a prisoner!" "You were a slave to sin and death, but I have the keys to set you free," Jesus said as he held them up for Josh to see.

Then he began to clean Josh's heart. He wiped down the walls and mopped the floors, bagged up the trash, and replaced all the old dirty and worn out furniture with beautiful brand new furniture. He went from room to room cleaning everything, big and small, nothing went untouched. It was amazing how quickly he worked. "Hey Josh, can you come here, please?" Jesus called out. "Do you remember this sin?" He asked, while holding up an old shoe. "No, should I?" Josh asked. "Think back to when you and Kyle were in sixth grade and the boy named Seth that you always picked on. This is the shoe that you had on when you kicked him. Now do you remember?" Jesus asked. "Oh no, you saw me

9

do that?" he was mortified. "We were so mean to that kid. We bullied him the whole year until he finally moved away. I feel so ashamed of myself, and I'm so sorry for the bad things I've done. Will you please forgive me Lord?"

I do forgive you son, and I'm putting that shoe and all of the other sin from your past and all the ones you'll commit in the future into this garbage bag and I'll throw it so far away we'll never see it again!" Jesus assured him. "Why do people sin? Why do we do such bad things to each other?" Joshua asked as he stared out the window. "It's not what I created you for, and it's not the way it should be. I hate sin and what it does to the world, the sorrow and pain it causes all of you," Jesus said sadly. "So, why did you let it happen, you could have stopped it, couldn't you?" Josh asked. "I wanted all of you to be free to choose to obey me or not to obey me. And I would never force you to love me, I didn't want robots! So, because I loved you so much, I gave you a free will," Jesus explained. "Can you tell me how it began, I mean, wasn't it Adam and Eve's fault?" Josh asked.

"Be quiet Josh, they'll hear you!" Jesus whispered as he pulled Josh behind a bush. He pointed to a man and woman who weren't wearing any clothes. They were standing under a tree in the distance but Josh could clearly see them. He blushed and quickly turned his head away. "Is that who I think it is?" he asked in a loud whisper. "Yes, it's Adam and Eve," Jesus answered. "They are about to eat the fruit from the tree that I warned them about," He explained. Joshua stood up and yelled, "HEY STOP THAT!" "Sit down Josh!" Jesus said sternly, as he pulled him back down. "But, they're going to ruin everything!" Josh complained. "The damage has already been done. Sin has entered the world through their disobedience. But my Father gave his only Son to take the punishment and pay the huge price for the sin of the whole world. The world is guilty, the son is innocent. The world is sinful and dirty, the Son is holy, clean and pure. He didn't have to save mankind, but He wanted to. I love the world so much and wanted to save all of you." Joshua thought about it for a while, and then he asked, "I thought you were Jesus?" "I am the Holy Spirit of God, the three of us are one." Josh didn't quite understand, but he didn't question him about it. "What happens to those who don't believe in you?" he asked. "If they don't choose to believe in me, they choose eternal separation from me," Jesus explained. "Does that mean they will go to Hell?" Josh asked. "That is the only place where I will not be, so yes," Jesus said sadly. "But why did you make such a terrible place?" Josh asked. "It's a place of eternal punishment created for Satan and the fallen angels," Jesus explained.

"I died so people would not have to go there. I gave all I could give to save mankind. There must be a choice, and there must be justice. If they don't want me to pay for their sin, then they must pay for it themselves." "Is there any other way to be saved?" Josh asked. "No, I am the only way of salvation. No one can work their way to Heaven or buy their way in. I am the way, the truth and the life. No one comes to the Father except through me," He explained. "I let you come into my heart and I've accepted your gift of salvation, will that get me into Heaven someday?" Josh asked. "You're in Josh, trust me!" Jesus assured him.

Then just as suddenly as they'd gone, they were back in the house. Josh looked around and said, "Thank you for cleaning the place up, I hardly recognize it! When I first saw it, it looked good to me. But it changed when you came in, it looked horrible. Why is that?" Josh asked. "When I came, I let you see the real condition of your heart and you needed to know how bad sin looks to me," Jesus explained. "One more thing, how did we time travel back to the Garden of Eden?" Josh asked. "Okay, A- this is a dream, and B- I'm God, I can do anything! Stick with me kid, and you'll be amazed at what I'll show you," Jesus said as he pulled a leaf out of Josh's hair.

Then Jesus picked up the heavy garbage bags and headed out the door. "I'll be right back. I've got to get this garbage out of here." "Thanks again Lord, it feels so great to be forgiven and free," Josh said with a smile. "I'm glad you let me come in son," Jesus smiled and walked out. The screen door closed with a loud bang.

Josh woke with a jerk. He rubbed his eyes and looked around his room. "*Wow! That was the best dream I've ever had!*" he thought. "*And I remember every detail. That never happens!*" He smiled to himself and sighed, "*I wish it were real.*"

3

⁓⚏⁓

The Study Room

Josh was feeling hungry so he quietly crept down to the kitchen to find something to eat. He saw the fried chicken and mashed potatoes his mom had saved for him. After warming it up, he sat alone in the dim light thinking about his dream. "What cha eating?" he heard his sister ask as she entered the kitchen. Josh nearly jumped off his chair, "you scared the, I mean you scared me!" He caught himself before he swore. "Sorry!" she giggled. "Is there any milk left?" she asked. "Yeah, there is, pour some for me too, will you? Then I have to tell you about the dream I had," he said. "Okay" she said as she mixed some chocolate in the milk and then sat across from him, "what did you dream about?" He proceeded to tell her every detail of his dream. "That's cool. I didn't know you thought much about God." "Well, I didn't before he showed up in my dream! But if God is like the guy in my dream, I would like to get to know Him. He's really nice and he's easy to talk to, not the way I used to picture him, you know?" "Yeah, I've always thought He was mad at me for the things I've done and for not going to church or feeding the poor and stuff," she said. "It sounds like He's really cool, not some big, mean God who sits up in the clouds somewhere. So are you and this dude Jesus going to be BFFs?" she kidded. "I don't think you should call God a dude," Josh laughed. "I'm going to bed, if you see him again, tell him I said hi," she laughed.

"Maybe He'll be in your dreams tonight," Josh said. "That would be so weird," she laughed. As she was heading back to her room, Josh smiled to think that he had gotten to talk to her. She used to be very outgoing but lately she hadn't been hanging out with any of her old friends and she just seemed so down all the time. He was going to try to talk to her about what was bothering her, but he didn't know how to bring it up. Maybe he could take her to a movie soon and spend some time with her. He chugged his milk down, belched, put his plate and cup in the dishwasher and then headed up to his room. *"I wish I could dream more about my house,* he thought as he fluffed his pillow and yawned.

"Hey Joshua, would you come down here?" Jesus yelled up the stairs. *"Oh my gosh! He's back!"* Josh thought as he raced down the steps. "Hi Jesus, I'm so glad you're here!" "Well, hello there, did you have a nice snack?" It was a cozy little room that looked like it could be a college professor's library. Two leather reading chairs completed the look. "Come over here and I'll show you where I was born." Jesus was sitting at the computer looking at a map of Israel. "Oh, I know that! It was the little town of Bethlehem, right?" Josh was proud of himself for knowing the answer. "That's right Josh!" Jesus said. "I've heard that a million times in Christmas carols," Josh admitted. Jesus smiled up at him, "here, sit down and I'll show you more."

"Now click there, that's the town of Nazareth. I grew up there. The man who helped to raise me…." "Joseph" Josh interrupted. "Yes and my mother." "Mary! Everyone knows her name." Josh said. "Okay, who is my real father?" Jesus asked. "Your real father is God," Josh said as he turned to look at Jesus. "You really are half man and half God, aren't you?" "No Josh, I'm fully man and fully God." "Wow!" was all Josh could think to say. "Why would you leave Heaven and come here to become one of us? And why did you choose a poor teen aged girl to be your mother? You should have been born in a palace, instead of a stable?"

Jesus smiled and said, "Love is gentle, love is kind. It is not puffed up. It doesn't want fan-fare, love only wants to give. I left the glory of Heaven for you. I was born humbly and lived as a servant to show you how to live. I gave everything for you, even my life because I love you!" Josh was speechless by this time, and he saw that Jesus had tears in his eyes.

Jesus had a way of making Josh feel what he was feeling, so he got a little choked up too. "I'd like to meet with you here each day Josh, so I can teach you from my word. Would you like that too?" Jesus asked. "That would be great! I like talking with you about all of this. I have a lot to learn, I mean I know a little about you, but I have to admit that I'm kind of new at all of this stuff," Josh said honestly. "Hey, I'll get you up to speed in no time! I'm just glad you want to learn. But, what I'd really like is to spend time with you and be your friend," Jesus said with a big smile on his face. "You can be my BFF!" Josh said and they both laughed. They then talked about their childhood homes and their families. "Hey Jesus, did your sisters and brothers know you were God in the flesh? I bet they were jealous because you were so perfect all the time? My parents thought my big brother was perfect too, boy, were they wrong! Did you show them your power when you were a kid? I bet you wanted to! I know I wanted to smite my brother a few times!"

As they talked, silent watchers were looking on, invisible to Josh's eyes at the time. They were the guardians who lived to serve their Lord and protect the humans living on earth all through the ages. They were listening and remembering the birth of their creator God. And they had marveled at witnessing the Son of God as he became flesh and lived among men.

"Oh Josh, you have some things on your computer that I don't want you to look at anymore. Will you get rid of them?" Jesus asked. "Ah, sure, I'll do that tomorrow," Josh promised. "Let's just take care of that now, shall we?" "CLICK" "NO!" Josh cried. "Does this mean you're going to change everything in my life?" he asked. "Can't I decide what stays and what goes? I'm not that bad, am I?" he asked in frustration. "You do need to be careful with what you look at and what you think about. It really does matter because as a man thinks in his heart, so is he," Jesus said. "Fill your mind with good things and soon you'll find yourself doing those good things. And if you do those good things long enough, it will develop a Godly character in you. You'll become more like me!" Jesus said. "I guess you're right, I really shouldn't be looking at that garbage. It makes me feel a little guilty when I do," Josh admitted. The two of them spent hours searching the web for good and inspirational stories and some funny ones too. Josh had no idea that talking to God could be so much fun. He found that he was beginning to feel a change in the way he thought. He wondered if he would feel the same tomorrow. But for now he was enjoying himself and his new friend.

After Jesus and Josh finished watching a funny animal video, Jesus turned to Josh and said, "I didn't delete anything Josh." "You didn't?" Josh looked confused. "It's your choice, I want you to decide if you will get rid of it or not. I'm not going to force you to," Jesus said. Josh thought about it for a moment, "you know what… I don't want that junk on my computer anymore and he decided to clean it out. "You made an excellent choice Josh!" Jesus said as he patted him on the shoulder. "Besides, who wants to watch all that stuff when you can watch cute little babies playing with kittens, right?" "*Yeah, sure, I'm going to watch kittens and puppies, you bet!*" Josh thought. "*He's going to try to make me do the things he likes to do. How can I tell him that I don't like this kind of stuff?*" Josh's mind was wandering. "Would you rather see some motor cross videos? Wait a minute, check this out! It's a Great White shark jumping out of the water!" Jesus said. "Cool, he caught that seal in mid-air! Now, that's more like it!" Josh laughed.

4

---❈---

The Kitchen and Dining Room

They stayed in the study for a long time and Josh began to feel a little hungry so he asked, "Are you hungry Jesus?" "Yes, I am," he answered. "I cook you know." "Good, a God who creates everything and can cook too! You're perfect!" Josh laughed. With that, they headed upstairs. Jesus really knew his way around a kitchen and in no time they were ready to eat. Josh had found the plates and silverware to set the table. They decided to eat in the kitchen where the afternoon sun was shining through the window. Jesus made broiled fish and steamed vegetables and Josh made some fresh lemonade for them to drink. "This tastes great, for healthy food," Josh said as he took more fish from the platter. "Thank you!" Jesus replied. "You did a good job making all the things we eat. I especially like cheeseburgers and chocolate shakes!" Josh said. "I'm glad you enjoy it all, I designed the best foods for you to eat, like fresh fruits, grains, nuts and vegetables. All of those are full of the nutrients and vitamins your body needs, but I also considered how they would look, smell and taste to you," Jesus said. "Think about the beauty of a strawberry, the smell of a peach and how a pineapple tastes in your mouth. I made everything with you in mind." *"Man, he sure put a lot of thought into his creation, and it's all good, but I think he wants me to eat nuts and berries all the time. Maybe he's a health fanatic! There goes my chili dogs and ice cream!"* Josh thought. Jesus heard his thoughts and said, "I allow you the freedom to eat what you want. You can eat meat and ice cream, just be wise about it. Everything is permitted but not everything is beneficial to you, remember your body is the Temple of God," He said as he finished his lemonade. "Ah, that was good, you make great lemonade Josh!" "Thanks, I couldn't have done it if you hadn't made the lemons!" Josh said, still thinking about the "Temple of God" remark.

"Is it okay with you if I just say thank you when I pray over the food?" "Of course it is! That's how I like it!" Jesus replied. "A sincere thank you from your heart is what I want, not a bunch of empty words and repetition that means nothing to you or me. You've always had a thankful heart Josh, I've listened to you all these years giving me the honor and credit for what I have made," he added. "I guess I did always believe in you, or I wanted to," Josh replied. Then Jesus laughed to himself. "What's so funny?" Josh asked. "Oh, this fish reminds me of the time Peter cooked lunch on the shore of Galilee. A piece of fish caught on fire; he flipped it off the rock and onto Thomas's blanket! Burned a big hole right through it! Peter never heard the end of it!" Jesus laughed as he thought about it. "I wish I could meet those guys! It sounds like you had a lot of fun together," Josh said. "We did have a lot of good times together, and don't worry you will get to meet them," Jesus said patting Josh's hand. "Soon we'll all be together sitting at my big table eating and laughing and enjoying one another's company!" "That will be great "BURP" Oh, excuse me!" Josh laughed. "That means you really liked it!" Jesus laughed. That was the first of many times that he and Josh would break bread together.

Josh heard a beeping sound. "Will you excuse me for a minute Joshua? I need to take this call." Jesus stood up and answered the phone. "Well hello there, Melissa!" He said cheerfully. Josh thought it was odd that Jesus would use a cell phone to talk to people. He was clearly interested in His friends and made each one of them feel important. "*I am amazed that He loves us all so much. He takes time to meet with us one on one and talk to us privately. He's such a good God and I'm glad he's my friend.*" He thought to himself.

As Josh started to do the dishes, he thought he heard the phone ringing again, but it wasn't the phone, it was his alarm clock and the loud noise woke him up. After he got his bearings he leaned over and turned it off. He stretched and let out a loud yawn as he looked up at the ceiling. *"I know that was real, there's no way that was just a dream!"* He smiled to think that he had just spent a day with God, dream or not, it was real to him. He grabbed his clothes and headed for the shower. Then he looked up again, *"are you there Jesus? "I'm right here Josh,* he heard the Holy Spirit respond in his head. "I heard that! You really are in my heart, I know you are!" He said out loud. "I'll see you tonight in my dreams, right?" *"I'll be there!"* Jesus responded.

He came down the stairs in a great mood, "good morning mom! I'm really sorry about last night," he said as he kissed her on the cheek." She laughed, "Well, good morning to you!" "What happened over night, were you switched by aliens? Are you really my son?" she laughed as she examined him closely. "I know I've been a jerk lately, and I'm so sorry for the way I've talked to you." He didn't wait for a response but continued, "can I be honest with you mom?" he asked, sitting down across from her. "Of course, tell me what's on your mind," she said. He slowly opened up about his feelings and he told her why he was so frustrated and angry with her. Then he went on to talk to her about his feelings toward his dad. She sat in silence for a long time just staring out the window but listening to everything he said. Josh began to think that he had said too much. Then his mom spoke, "honey, I've got something to tell you." He didn't say a word, he just sat and waited for her to compose herself and speak. "I haven't been completely honest with you kids about your dad," she stopped to wipe back some tears, "it's been two years since we've seen him and I've been lying about the whole situation."

"What are you talking about, tell me?" Josh was anxious to learn the truth. "You told us dad was doing something for the government, something so important that he couldn't even let us know and that he would be gone for years working on it. Was that all a lie?" "I didn't know what else to tell you." She hesitated to say anything more, fearing his reaction "I lied about it to protect your dad's image. I didn't want you to think badly of him. Then one lie led to another and another. The truth is…. your dad was arrested two years ago for smuggling drugs into Saudi

Arabia." "WHAT! That can't be true!" Josh yelled and stood up. "I never believed it either Josh! And I've tried and tried to get someone to help me contact him so I can find out the truth. Our own government can't seem to get any answers either!" She said. "What about the money, I thought he was sending you money all this time?" Josh asked. "That was another lie, I'd been using the money from our savings but it ran out and that's why I had to go to work, to cover living expenses. It isn't enough though, I'm way behind on the bills." She hated to worry him with that news. Josh sat down hard as if a heavy load of bricks had fell on him.

"The worst thing is that no one knows where he is. He just disappeared, so did Bobby, apparently he was in on it too." She said. (Bobby was a good friend.) "So let me get this straight, dad and Bobby weren't working for the oil company, they were smuggling drugs?" Josh said as he stood up again. "No, he was working. The man that contacted me from your dad's company was really surprised because your dad was one of his best workers. It doesn't make any sense to me, it's not like your dad at all!" she said.

She admitted that she had moments of doubt, wondering if it were true about the drugs, and if it were true, she wondered how Derek could have changed so much. She and Derek had a good marriage and their love remained strong, even when he had to work far away. He had always been an honest man, a loyal friend and a wonderful father. "I've tried to get answers from the Saudi government through senators and diplomats but no one seemed to know what happened to them. I was just about to tell you and make all of this public, I was thinking of trying to go on television because I couldn't get anyone else to help me, when I got a call from Bobby," she said with a change in her tone. "He said he's back home, in this country, and he wants to come here to tell me something in person! He said it was good news but he didn't want to talk about it over the phone," she said excitedly. Josh knew that his mom had just shared stuff that she had held inside for a long time, and he wasn't sure how to respond to her. He walked over and gave her a big hug which surprised them both. "Thanks for telling me mom, but I don't know why you thought we shouldn't know about it, we could have helped you! I'm not sure what to think about dad now. I don't know how I feel towards him yet. It's hard to know what to believe." He paused then asked, "When will Bobby be here?" "He said he would call when he gets in town. I want you and Bethany here with me when he comes. No more secrets or lies, I promise!" She felt relieved to tell him. "Can you forgive me Josh? I am so sorry for lying to you and for leaving you alone so many nights," she pleaded. "Of course I forgive you, now I know why you had to work, it was because of him! He's the one who did this to us!" Josh said angrily. Cami didn't know what to say to that because sometimes she had felt the same way. After they had talked about it for a while, Josh began to tell her about his dreams. "I'll talk to you about it more when I get home," he said as he kissed her good bye. "Thank you for telling me mom, it changes the way I feel about you." His mood had changed so many times that morning and he left feeling dazed and confused.

It was Saturday and he had to mow and trim the cemetery grass. His mom had helped him get the job because she knew the wife of the grounds keeper. Josh was trimming around the graves of Henry and Margret Cook who were people, he imagined, that were pretty important around here back in the 1800s, considering the size of their tombstones. Josh's ancestors had lived in this area at that time as well. His family on his dad's side had originally come from Germany. They moved to the mid-west in the early 1800's. His ancestors on his mother's side were originally from Sweden, they also settled in the area in that time frame, so Josh had roots in this part of the country. He tried to picture what Angel Cross had looked like back in those days. Once a week, the small local newspaper had a historic picture printed on the front page of the paper and a story to go along with it. Josh had always discarded the papers, but now he was beginning to take an interest in the local history and he wished he'd have kept them.

He was happily thinking about the past and what it must have been like when his thoughts suddenly did a U-turn back to his dad. He really wanted some answers and he could hardly wait to hear what Bobby had to tell them. He was deep in thought when he glanced up. What he saw across the street grabbed his complete attention, it was Kayla and her friend Darcy walking into the hair salon which was in the old brick building that had once been a drug store. Kayla was the girl that Josh had day dreams about. He had only talked to her a few times at football games when his school played hers but there was something about her that made her stand out from the other girls he knew. He felt his heart skip because she turned toward him and smiled. "*She smiled at me! He* thought as he turned to see if anyone else was around. *Yep, it was me she smiled at, not you dead guys*". He stood there for a moment just staring at the building, wondering how long it would take her to get her hair done. As he returned to his trimming he started to formulate a plan to ask her out. *What should I do Jesus?* He surprised himself by asking God for dating advice. "*Just ask her Josh, she won't bite!*" He heard an inner voice say. "*Yeah, what's the worst that can happen? She smiled after all, that's a good sign. But what should I take her to do?*" he wondered. That's when he remembered what his mom had told him about girls, "Just keep it simple, and be yourself. Let her get to know the real you." "*That's it, something fun but simple. We can go for a walk and maybe get some ice cream. Or should I ask her out for dinner? Nah, I'll save that for the second date, I better start saving my money!*" he thought.

"Hey Josh, can you hear me?" He turned to see Kayla and her friend standing on the sidewalk in front of the cemetery waving at him. He turned off the trimmer, and waved back as he walked toward them. "Hi, I saw you go in the hair place, it looks like they do good work in there because you look great!" he said. "Oh, well, thank you, actually we just stopped there to get the shampoo I like. I didn't know you worked here," she said. "Yeah, every Saturday morning I'm here. I work at Cowboy Joe's too," he said. "Cowboy Joe's, I love their cheeseburgers!" "Me too," he laughed "and we have the world's best chocolate fudge cake!" For some reason it was easier to talk to her now. He remembered how awkward he used to feel around her and he cringed when he thought about what had happened a year earlier. He had heard some big guy yelling crude remarks at her and her friend so he bravely told the guy to shut his mouth. The big guy stuffed Josh in a garbage can, head first! It surprised him that Kayla even remembered his name after that humiliating experience. But she was impressed and thought it was sweet of him to protect her ears from such bad language. Not knowing her last name, he lost track of her after that night. A year later he happened to see her in a powder blue Mustang headed in the opposite direction. He found out that she was working on a horse ranch just outside of town. After that he drove past the ranch once or twice a week hoping to see her outside with the horses, but he never found the courage to stop and talk to her. Now he had the opportunity so he thought it would be the perfect time to ask her out.

"Hey Kayla, I was wondering if you would like to get some ice cream later, and uh, maybe take a walk by the lake?" "Sure Josh that would be fun. What time?" she asked. He told her that he would be done mowing by noon. Since she was going to be shopping in town, she said she could meet him after that. "I'm glad you can go! How about we meet at the ice cream place at 1:00?" he asked. "I'll be there!" she promised. He smiled and waved as the girls walked away. "See you there!" he shouted. He put his hands on his head and felt the grass clippings in his hair, *"Ah, man, I've got grass all over me!"* He thought. *"But she's going out with me anyway!"*

The girls giggled as they walked away. "He's so cute!" Kayla whispered to her friend. Josh made sure she wasn't watching when he jumped up and gave a silent "YA-HOO!" He worked quickly so he could finish by noon. He raced home after work to shower and change. Back in his car, he drove to the ice cream shop. It was a beautiful place, the path along the lake was edged with trees and flowers all in bloom, there were new benches and old fashioned lampposts that had been added the summer before, small angel statues had been placed among the flowers here and there along the walkway, the park planners had also hired landscapers to create a rock garden with a lighted waterfall which added beauty and charm to the place. The harbor was busy with all kinds of boats coming in and going out. There were sail boats, speed boats, fishing boats and kayaks all filled with people who were enjoying the beautiful day. People were walking, running, riding bikes, and pushing strollers along the path. Some were swimming, some were picnicking, and others were playing catch. It was a little piece of Heaven and it was about to get even better, Josh thought. He pulled into the parking lot and looked for Kayla's car. She was parked under a cherry tree, a blue car with pink fuzzy dice hanging from the rear view mirror. He spotted her near the lake surrounded by a group of children. He sat in his car a few minutes and watched her playing a game of tag with them. "Oh good, she likes kids," he said out loud.

Their first date was everything Josh hoped it would be, a long walk down the path, just talking and getting to know each other. They'd ordered ice cream, which they barely touched. It seemed they were more interested in talking than eating. Kayla talked about school and mentioned that her senior prom was coming up, but Josh totally missed the hint. He told her all about his baseball team, his jobs and a little bit about his dreams for the future. They were having a great time and Josh hadn't once thought about his dad. They had spent hours together and the time flew by, it was getting late in the afternoon, Kayla had to go back to the stables for something. It was hard for them to say good bye. "I'm so glad I saw you today," she said. "You have no idea how long I've wanted to do this Kayla!" Josh said "and this..." he took her hand and held it to his lips. He closed his eyes and kissed it softly. "Oh, how sweet, nobody does that anymore!" she whispered. "This was a special day Josh, thank you!"

On the way home, Josh thought about everything Kayla had said, everything she had done, the clothes she wore, the way she looked, it was so perfect! *"I think I'm in love already!"* he thought to himself. *"I'm proud of you Joshua! You treated her like a lady. She is very special to me, and I want you to respect her."* Josh heard the voice of the Holy Spirit whisper." *If that was you Lord, I want you to know that I feel the same way!"* He responded in his thoughts. The voice in his head made him think. *"I wonder if that's just my thoughts or could it really be God speaking to me?"*

When he got home, he grabbed a sandwich and a drink and headed for the deck. He sat there thinking about everything that had happened that day. His mom called his cell phone and left a message, "Josh, don't forget to mow the yard and take out the garbage, thank you honey!" she said. He normally argued about it or put it off, but he suddenly felt like he should be helping her more, after all, she had worked hard to support the family, with no help from his dad. Thinking about that made him mad. *"I can't believe he's a stupid drug smuggler! Way to go dad! Thanks for missing two years of my life because you're an idiot!"* he thought.

Josh did the things his mom had asked him to do without complaining. He fixed the loose gate hinge and raked up some old leaves that were under the bushes and in the flower beds. He even brought out the patio furniture from the storage room behind the garage knowing that it would make her happy. She always had to beg him to do things like that, it felt good to do something nice for her without having to be asked first. It got him thinking about how much she did for everyone else and she rarely complained about it, she just did it because she loved her family. That's when Josh decided that he would never take her hard work for granted again.

Cami was a personal assistant and care giver for an older gentleman named Isaac Jacobson. She cooked his meals, cleaned his house, took him to the doctor and to the store, but most of the time he just wanted her to keep him company. Isaac was Jewish and he liked to share his faith and culture with anyone who would listen; Cami didn't mind that at all, she had always admired the Jewish people and their history. She really enjoyed talking with him about bible stories; sometimes she would slip one in about Jesus and his disciples. He didn't object to hearing about Cami's faith and he found it fascinating when she tried to convince him that Jesus was the Messiah that the Jews had been waiting for. He thought her arguments were very compelling.

Isaac trusted her so much that he had confided in her about a dark time in his life. As a child, he had witnessed the Holocaust and some of the members of his family had been killed by the Nazis. Ironically, Isaac's second wife was of German decent. He was not in the least bit bitter over the past, preferring to forgive his enemies and live in peace and knowing that his German wife had nothing at all to do with it. He had loved her and her son Phillip dearly and he treated him and his children like they were his own flesh and blood. He was invited to stay with Phillip and his family in Florida for three weeks, so he gave Cami the time off with pay! She had two weeks left of her vacation time and she planned to take Josh and Bethany on a little get away before it ended. They all needed to do something different, something fun. Ever since she had become a Christian she had dreamed of visiting Israel, the land of the bible, but a trip like that wasn't in her budget. She would have to settle for a week end at the Pine View hotel; at least it had a pool and game room for the kids and a hot tub and lounge chairs for her.

Josh sat on the deck sipping on some cold water and thinking about his mom. From now on he was going to help her more and he would even give her part of his pay check every week. It was time that he paid his fair share. Then it hit him square in the face, he wasn't a boy any more, he was a man. At the end of the day he felt different about things, he felt better than he had felt in a long time and stronger too. He felt like a new person inside, and he was! He went up to his room, took a shower, checked his messages, then he fell asleep thinking about his day.

5

The Living Room

"She's a great girl," Jesus said as they walked into the living room. "I really like her, and I think she may be the one for me, we have so much in common," Josh responded. "That was fast!" Jesus laughed. Josh started a fire in the fireplace which began to warm up the room. Then he sat down to visit with his new best friend. He glanced over at the television and started thinking about it, *"I wonder if Jesus likes to watch television. I bet he won't want to watch the violent stuff I watch, most of it is pretty bad and it would be embarrassing to watch those shows with him here. I wonder if he'll make me watch "Little house on the Prairie" and boring junk like that? And he probably doesn't like football."* He looked up to see Jesus smiling at him. "Yes Josh, I like to watch football, we'll discuss the other shows later." Josh blushed "I forgot you know what I'm thinking." "Yeah, better think about what you're thinking about!" Jesus kidded.

Jesus pulled a book off the shelf and sat back in the large leather chair and put his feet up. He started to read then he said something strange, "Is Satan prowling around again? Get rid of him!" Josh somehow knew that he wasn't talking to him. "Am I going to be alright?" he asked. "Fear not," was all Jesus said in response. Josh looked around the room and didn't see anyone and Jesus seemed calm and peaceful as he read his book. *"Well, if he's not worried, I won't worry either,"* he thought. "Satan is looking for a way to enter your home," Jesus said without looking up. "What, you mean he wants to come in here? You won't let him in, will you?" Josh asked nervously. "I've closed all the entrances to your heart,

29

but stay alert because he'll keep trying to find a breach in your character and he knows where your weakest points are. All he needs is a small crack in the wall to sneak in." "I have weak points? Where are they, I mean, what are they?" Josh asked, alarmed at the news. "One weak point is located in your mouth, that's where lies jump off your tongue." Josh pictured a diving board. "You don't lie often, but enough to allow Satan to stick his nose in your business. He loves to hear you tell lies because he's the "Father of all Lies. He'll surf right in on a wicked wave of falsehoods which can easily become a filthy tsunami of deceit. I detest lies!" Jesus said, almost spitting out the words. "Oh, I'll never let Satan get in here, I'll never tell another lie, I promise!" Josh said confidently. "He's sneaky Josh, if you give him an inch, he'll take a mile, or even ten miles!" Jesus laughed. "He'll try to convince you that one little sin won't hurt you, but remember this," Jesus leaned toward Josh and spoke in a serious tone, "sin may seem fun for a while, but it will always lead you down a path of destruction. It's like a stairway, each step down takes you closer to the bottom…. and you don't want to go there Josh, there's nothing good in the basement of your heart!" Jesus sternly warned. He smiled at Josh then sat back, returning to his book. Josh also sat back in his chair and thought about what he had just heard, *the basement, I don't think I ever want to see the basement, it sounds really creepy!*" He shivered at the thought of what might be lurking down there. He tried to think of something more pleasant. "Hey Jesus, do you know what's going to happen with me and Kayla?" "I sure do!" Jesus said with a smile. With that smile, Josh was sure everything would work out just fine, so he asked no more questions about it.

He walked over to the book shelf and searched for something funny or wholesome to read, anything that would take his mind off of "the basement!" Smiling like he had just seen an old friend, he pulled a familiar book off the shelf, thumbed through it and decided to read it, again!

The book Josh was reading started to make him feel a little funny, like he was melting or something. He stopped reading for a moment and looked at Jesus, "did you feel that?" he asked. "Feel what?" Jesus asked. "It felt like I was being pulled into this story, weird huh?" he said. "Try putting your hand over the last paragraph you read," Jesus suggested. Josh said "Okay, now what?" Jesus responded saying, "close your eyes and listen." Josh did as Jesus said, then he opened his eyes quickly when he heard a girl screaming, "PA, COME QUICK! LAURA FELL DOWN THE WELL!" He spun around and saw a young girl in a long dress and wearing braids running toward him. "Oh no you didn't!" he gasped as he glanced down at his long boots and suspenders. "You changed me into Charles Ingalls?!" He knew the characters well because his mother had read him all of the books when he was a child. Josh was horrified by the thought. "Pa, come quick!" The girl cried. "I'm not your Pa!" he protested. She pulled on his arm, "you have to help her Pa! She'll drown down there!" "Oh, okay I'm coming! Show me where she is!" The thought of Laura drowning made him panic a little, he ran after the frantic girl as she led the way. They ran over the hill and through a pasture when he heard a scream for help echoing out of the stone well. They were both out of breath as they reached the well. "Laura, Pa's here, he'll get you out!" the girl reassured her. "Pa, I'm afraid don't leave me!" Laura cried. "I'll get a rope half pint, you hang on now!" Josh's couldn't help himself from speaking like Pa, it's like he was possessed by Pa! His eyes widened as he saw how deep and dark the well was. "Mary, go fetch your mother!" Josh said as he tried to look for a rope or something to pull Laura out with. He spotted a chain on the ground near the barn. He grabbed it and ran to the tree by the well. He wrapped the chain around a thick oak tree and fastened it together with a piece of wire. "*Now what?*" he asked himself. "Pa, the water is getting higher! I hurt my hand and my leg, I can't stand much longer! Please help me!" she cried. "I'm coming half pint, hold on!" he yelled.

Josh wrapped the chain around his waist and crawled over the edge of the well. "Here I come, Laura!" He began to repel himself down the well, suddenly his feet slipped off the crumbly limestone rocks and he was dangling from the chain which was cutting into his wrists. He began to sweat and shake as it was more difficult than he thought it would be. "PA, BE CAREFUL!" Laura shrieked. Josh got his balance and his footing on the rocks then slowly he began to lower himself down again. *"How deep is this thing?"* he wondered. His hands were throbbing with the pain and the weight he was holding. *"God, how am I going to lift her out, I can barely hold myself up? Please help me!"* he silently prayed. *"I am with you. I will give you the strength you need,"* Jesus assured him. Josh finally reached the bottom, "oh Pa, you made it!" Laura cried as she hugged him. Josh was surprised by his reaction, he got all teary eyed and hugged her back, "let's get you out of here!" he said. "Climb up on my shoulders." "But Pa, I'm too heavy!" she said. "We can do this, God will help us," Josh said. So Laura did as she was told and climbed up and sat on his shoulders. Josh mustered all the strength he had and hand over hand he slowly, painfully began to climb. Halfway up his foot slipped off the wall. Laura let out a scream. "Hold on Laura!" Josh said as he struggled to get a stable footing, his shoulder and arms were aching but he was determined to get them out of that well. All of a sudden he heard voices. "Charles, Laura, we're coming!" Joshua looked up to see Caroline with a couple of strong looking men looking down at him. "I brought help!" she called down to him.

The two farmers grabbed the chain with their huge hands and began to pull Laura and Josh up. They reached down and lifted Laura off of Josh's shoulders. Then they easily pulled Josh up and out. He collapsed on the ground all wet and shaking, everyone rushed to him and Laura and hugged them. "Oh Pa, thank you, you saved me!" Laura cried. Josh was crying by now and hugging this family as if it was his own. "I love you half pint!" he cried. He opened his eyes and found himself on his knees hugging a pillow from his chair. "Huh, Jesus, how did that happen? It felt so real, like I was really there with Laura and her family. I could actually feel the pain!" He examined his wrists and saw no blood, not even a scratch. "Now do you think you might want to watch "Little house on the Prairie?" Jesus asked with a wink. "Yeah, I think I do, I'm part of their family now!" he laughed. "Good, we'll start with season one," Jesus laughed. Josh sighed.

Josh stood up and walked over to the book shelf. As he looked over the titles of the books he asked, "Would I be able to enter into any of these stories?" "Which one interests you the most?" Jesus asked. Josh took a few books off of the shelf and brought them to Jesus. He chose non-fiction books about history, one was about European explorers, one was about the Pilgrims and one was about the Lewis and Clark expedition. "Ah, history, that's a very good choice, but are you really sure you want to experience these things? I know that most of the people who lived through these events wouldn't want to go through them again; it was harder than you think! On the other hand, they did press on and overcame their fears, making it past the hardships and because they did, it opened up a whole new world to them!" Jesus said. "I think it would be fun. Can you give me a couple of minutes in this one?" He asked, handing Jesus the book that was in his hand. Jesus took it and read the cover and laughed, "You're brave to pick that one! Are you sure you want to do this?" "I'm sure, let's start at the beginning!" Josh said, closing his eyes and holding his breath.

When he opened his eyes everything was dark. "I'm here Joshua, are you ready?" Jesus asked. "I think so," Josh said nervously. "All right then," Jesus appeared out of the darkness as if he had been standing behind it. He looked into Josh's eyes with pure holiness and love. Then he spoke these words, not loudly but in a whisper…….. "LET THERE BE LIGHT!"

6

The Work Shop

After all that excitement, Josh felt like doing something calmer. "I think I saw a work shop downstairs, want to build something with me? I know you're a carpenter Jesus," he said. "Sure, let's check it out," Jesus said as he sat the book down. In the workroom, Josh rubbed his hands together eagerly and said, "What should we build first? Maybe we can build a chest for my friend Karly and her baby?" Karly had been Josh's friend ever since they met in the second grade. "Hold your horses Josh, first we need to build your foundation." Jesus said. "Huh? What do you mean?" Josh asked. "I'm the rock," Jesus said. "What's the rock?" Josh asked, looking confused. "I am." Jesus replied. "You're a rock?" Josh asked. "I'm solid and unchanging," Jesus explained. "Oh, duh, I should have known that," Josh chuckled. "Let me tell you a story," Jesus said as he sat down on a stool. "There was a wise man who built his house on a rock." "On you, right?" Josh interrupted. "Yes, anyone who hears my word and does what it says is wise." Suddenly Josh and Jesus were standing on a cliff overlooking the ocean. With the wind blowing through their hair, Jesus continued the story using the incredible visuals before them. "And down there, he pointed to the beach below, the foolish man built his house on the sand." Jesus had to yell above the sound of the wind and the crashing waves. "Anyone who hears my word but doesn't do what it says is foolish. When the storms come, the house on the rock will stand firm," Jesus said just as a horrific storm approached.

It started thundering and raining. The wind was so strong it almost blew Josh off his feet. He pointed to the house built on the sand. "Look! It's falling apart!" he yelled. "What's going to happen to the foolish man Lord?" "He wouldn't listen to me, no matter how hard I tried to warn him." Just then a big gust of wind knocked Josh to the ground. Jesus grabbed his arm and pulled him away from the edge of the steep cliff. Suddenly they were back in the workroom. "Whew! That was close! I nearly got blown off that cliff!" Josh said, breathing heavily. Then he smiled up at Jesus and said, "But I do like these adventures you take me on, they're awesome!" "Well, now do you understand why your foundation is so important?" Jesus asked. "Yes I do Lord. I want to build my house on you and on your word." "Atta boy Josh!" Jesus said, slapping Josh on the back in a friendly gesture. "Now hand me that Bible."

Jesus read the 5th and 6th chapter of the book of Matthew out loud. Joshua listened to every word carefully. "So, you want me to love everyone, even my enemies?" Josh asked. "Yes, it's easy to show love to those who love you back, but I want you to show love to those who are mean to you, even to those who hate you. And don't hold grudges against anyone, forgive and you will be forgiven. Of what you receive, give to help others, then it shall be given back to you in greater measure. Don't give to those who can repay you, but give and show mercy to those who can never repay you," Jesus said. "That goes against my nature," Josh admitted. "To do these things is to obey my word. My ways are higher than your ways Josh. Remember, when you do what I say, you are building your life on the rock." Jesus explained. "I'll try Lord, it won't be easy, but I'll try." "Good Josh, just one act of obedience at a time and you'll be building on a foundation will stand forever, for my word will never fade away. I am the same yesterday, today and forevermore." Joshua stood speechless at such majestic words. Finally he spoke, "What if I can't do it, what if I fail?"

"May I give you a test on this Josh?" Jesus asked. "Um, I guess so," Josh replied. "Okay, are you ready to forgive your dad? I know the times that he has hurt your feelings by not showing up for your games and how you think he doesn't care about what is going on in your life and in your sister's life. I've seen the tears of hurt and anger you've shed because he missed your birthday and your graduation ceremony," Jesus said as he put a comforting hand on Josh's shoulder. "Aw, I'm no baby! He didn't hurt my feelings," Josh said trying to act tough. "Joshua, I created you, don't you think I know you?" Jesus asked softly. "Let me show you something son." He said as he pulled out his extra, extra smart phone. "Here's your dad showing his friends your baseball team picture, and here he is at work talking about how much he misses his family."

Josh was surprised to see his dad actually talking about him. "But he's the one who messed up everything! Why did he do it, Lord? He wasn't here to help my mom. He wasn't here for anything for the past two years!" "That is something that you'll have to ask him," Jesus said. "I don't really care to see him, I'm mad at him and I don't think I can forgive him," Josh said. "Trust me to reach him Joshua, only I can change his heart and he might surprise you," Jesus said. "So, will you forgive him?" Joshua hung his head for a moment to think. "I don't know God, I'm too mad at him." He said. "Josh, what if I would have said that to you? What if I were too mad at you to forgive you?" Josh looked at Jesus with a frightened look on his face. "Don't worry, I have forgiven you. But are you greater than I am? If I am willing to forgive, shouldn't you also forgive?" Josh had hot tears rolling off his cheeks. "Let go of your anger and bitterness, give it to me Josh." Josh felt a heavy weight on his back and he saw leather straps buckled around his shoulders. "Give me your burden son," Jesus said as he held out his hands. Josh unbuckled the straps and let the heavy pack fall to the ground. "Forgive him for what he has done to you." Josh fell into the arms of his Heavenly Father and was comforted by his loving embrace. Then he bent over to pick up the pack, he handed it to Jesus and said, "I will forgive him Lord." With that, Jesus took the pack and threw it far away. Josh suddenly felt free of all the anger and bitterness that he had felt for so long. It made him feel as light as a feather. "It's gone, I'm free from it! What an amazing feeling!" All he could do was laugh with joy.

"Now replace the hurt feelings with love," Jesus put his hands on Josh's head. It was a warm sensation and Josh knew it was God's love flowing through him. His thoughts toward his dad felt buffered by this love, it was wonderful. Then Josh had a thought and he asked, "Jesus, you know everything, will you tell me where my dad is? Did he really sell drugs?" "I'm going to let this story unfold by itself. It'll be better that way. Just remember, all things work together for good for those who are mine."

After Jesus talked to Josh about foundations, he offered to help him work on the chest for Karly and her baby. "This will be very special to Karly, why don't I show you how to carve the baby's name on it?" "That'd be great! His name is Landon," Josh said. "Oh, I know his name Josh, I know him very well," Jesus said with a smile. "Of course you do, I forget that you made us all," Josh responded. "Landon is such a cute little guy and he's really smart. You know the future Lord, will Landon do something great someday? Will he succeed in life?" Josh asked. "That depends on how *you* measure success, I look at the heart to measure success. Landon will be a man after my own heart and even though he's a little baby, he's already my dear friend, just like you are!"

Josh smiled as he worked knowing that God had just called him his dear friend. "I like working with you Lord, and I am really enjoying the time we have together." "That's wonderful Josh. I want you to talk to me about everything. Let me be a part of all of your life, not just some of it. Many of my people only think of me at church and some only pray when they need my help. Please don't be like that Josh. I want to be welcomed into all the rooms of your heart." Jesus said as he worked on the chest. Josh thought about what Jesus had said for a while before he spoke. "Now that I know you Lord, I don't think I would ever want to do anything without you." "Guard your time with me, Josh. Satan will do everything in his power to distract you. Keeping you busy and distracted are his favorite tools," Jesus said as he held up a wrench to illustrate. Keeping yourself busy isn't bad at all. Just don't get so busy that you neglect our time together. I know many pastors who spend hours doing my work, but who spend very little time with me personally," he said soberly. "Really, there are pastors who don't spend time with you?" Josh was truly surprised by that. "Just be aware of it Josh. I am the vine, you are the branch, without me, you will wither away. So stay connected to me," Jesus warned. Josh looked at Jesus and with all seriousness said, "I will Lord."

When they finished working on the chest, they stood back to see what they had created together. It was beautiful and well made. "I didn't realize what a craftsman I was!" Josh said proudly. "But I couldn't have done it without you," he added. "She will be so surprised when I give it to her!" Then he had another idea, "I should fill it with baby things!" "Yeah, like diapers and bottles!" Jesus added. "And baby clothes and toys!" Josh was getting excited about the thought of helping his friend. "She has been asking for my help and provision, by giving her this, you are doing my work on earth. You have become my hands reaching out to those in need," Jesus said with a big smile on his face. "Well done!" Jesus helped Josh carry the wooden chest up the stairs. "I'll go shopping soon and fill it with gifts," Josh said. "Thanks again, Jesus. I can do anything with your help!" "That's not a random thought Josh, it's written in my word, and if it's written in my word, it's my promise to you. With me, you can do all things," Jesus said."

7

The Rec Room

"Hey Jesus, would you like to play a game of pool with me?" Josh asked. Surprisingly he was still full of energy. He was hoping that Jesus would say yes to him, but deep down he knew that playing games was something that God had no desire to do. Boy was he surprised and delighted when Jesus said yes! Josh was like a little kid when it came to playing sports and games, he loved them all. He ran up the stairs and yelled back to Jesus, "I'll beat you to the rec room!" When he got to the room he found Jesus was already there racking up the balls. "Hey there slow poke, you can break," Jesus kidded. "Sure, I'll break, are we playing eight ball?

As they played they talked. "Hey Jesus, do you like all the games and sports people play?" Josh asked. "I like most of them, but not the ones where they try to beat the living daylights out of each other! And I don't like the fact that so many people worship athletes and the games they play. Some people will pay almost anything for a ticket to a game, but they never give anything to help the poor. And it saddens me that many of my own people get more excited over a touchdown than they do about worshiping me," Jesus said as he knocked a ball into the side pocket. "I made you to be active and creative and I enjoy watching you have fun, I don't expect you to sit around all the time with nothing to do. I want your life to be abundant and fulfilling, but you'll never find total fulfillment in this world without me," he said, hitting a ball into the corner pocket. "You love competing and striving to win, I get that, but it's never enough. You like to build and create and you love to accomplish things because that's how I made you, all of you. That's why there'll be lots of projects and jobs for you to do in Heaven, and I've got millions of fun things planned for us," Jesus said. "Really, I've always pictured Heaven as one long church service with nothing to do but sing," Josh laughed. "Oh there will be a lot of singing going on, a lot of dancing and celebrating too!" Jesus said with a smile. "Now I can't wait to get there, I mean, I don't want to go there yet, but the way you describe it is getting me excited, tell me more! Will there be mountain biking and baseball in Heaven? How about water skiing and scuba diving, can we do those things too?" Josh asked fully expecting to hear him say no.

"Yes Josh, we'll do all that and more! And when you go scuba diving, you won't need to use an air tank to breathe," Jesus said as he chalked his cue stick. "What, how can that be?" Josh asked. He was more interested in the conversation than he was in the game. "Well Joshua, if I can walk on the water, what makes you think I won't let you walk with me under the water? Aren't I the one who created the water in the first place? Read Job 38:16 sometime," Jesus said. "Wow, that will be amazing!" Josh exclaimed. "My kingdom is a place of joy and wonder, a place where I will live with my people in perfect love and harmony. It's a place with no sin and no curse, a place where you are safe and free to be who I created you to be!" Jesus said. "Will there be children in Heaven?" Josh asked. "Oh yes, there are lots of children in my kingdom! The air is filled with their laughter and singing, I've made playgrounds that stretch for miles and the children are always happy and carefree as they play." Jesus said. "Will we eat in Heaven?" Josh asked. "Oh dear Joshua, do I have a party planned for you! It will be the most spectacular celebration there has ever been! Of course we will eat! What is a celebration without food? I promise you will never be bored or hungry in the Kingdom of Heaven!" Jesus said with a big smile on his face. "Try to imagine a place with no more war and no more sickness, no more hunger and where no one feels lonely. It is beyond your imagination!" Jesus said. "That sounds like an old song I've heard," Josh said. "Oh yeah, I know that song, and it doesn't include me. Some think that they can create their own utopia or paradise on earth. There is no way that mankind can create a beautiful and peaceful kingdom apart from me, they have tried and failed since the beginning of time. Only in my Kingdom will there be true peace and love among people," Jesus said as he called the corner pocket and knocked the eight ball into it.

The two of them then played a game of darts, which Jesus also won. "You're pretty good at playing pool and darts, was that the human side of you playing or the God part?" Josh laughed. "Now, don't be a sore loser Josh!" Jesus kidded. "Besides, if I wanted to, I could beat you with both hands tied behind the back of my "human side!" "That's not fair, you're God and I'm not!" Josh laughed. "Use the joy of the Lord, it's your strength," Jesus said. "Really, okay then watch this!" Josh started singing an old song he had learned in vacation bible school when he was little, "I've got the joy, joy, joy, joy down in my heart"......He bent down to pick up his weights "It's working, I feel stronger already!" He had no idea that an invisible spotter was standing behind him, just in case he needed a little assistance.

Josh woke up laughing out loud. He sat up and smiled at what he had just dreamed about. *"This is so cool, I love these dreams!"* he thought to himself. He went to the desk in his room and pulled out a tablet and pen and began to write it all down. Then he recalled in the dream how he had forgiven his dad. *"Oh no, he's not getting off that easy!"* he thought. When he stood up he felt stiff in his back and neck, he tried stretching but it didn't go away. By saying that, he had put the invisible weight back on his shoulders. He remembered what Jesus had said about forgiving his dad, but he decided to put it off for a while, at least until he found out what really happened. Little did Josh realize that Satan's minions were happily building a new addition to the fortress they had established in his mind, Satan was pleased to have gained more territory.

In the next room Josh heard his mother doing something. *"Oh, I almost forgot today is Sunday. I probably should go to church with her,"* he thought. *"That would totally freak her out!"* he laughed. He quickly got dressed and went to her door and knocked, "Hey mom, you going to church?" "Yeah, why?" she wondered. "Do you mind if I go with you?" There was a long pause because she was in shock. "Oh, yes, I'd like you to go with me!" she tried not to sound too surprised. "Should I ask Bethany to go too?" "Sure, that would be great, honey!" she said as she silently thanked God for preforming a miracle on her son. She tried not to be pushy with the kids about going to church, when they were younger they went willingly, but as they got older they refused to go. She tried to live her faith in God in front of them and they were watching her closely, noticing the changes in her since she had become a Christian. She had always been nice, but now she was super nice! Although, the kids had seen her "dark side" come out a few times, but she would always apologize and tell them, "God is still working on me!"

"Knock, knock, Hey Beth, do you want to go to church with me and mom?" Josh asked as he stood outside of her bedroom door. "You're going to church?" she sounded surprised. "That dream really messed with you, didn't it?" No answer came. "Oh just get up and come with us!" Josh begged. "No thanks." "Do it for me Beth, please!" he pleaded with a pathetic whine. "Ugh, alright I'll go, give me minute," she said, her heart slightly melting. Josh smiled and looked up, "Thank you God!" he whispered. He then asked his mom when they should tell Bethany about her dad, they both agreed they would tell her as soon as she came downstairs. Her reaction surprised them both because she acted like she couldn't care less. She was so unemotional about it that it got them worried. "What do you think about all of that Beth?" Josh asked. "I don't care, it's his life," she answered. "Wow, you really don't care! Aren't you mad at him at all?" he asked. "Why should I be, I think he has the right to do whatever he wants, it doesn't bother me one way or the other," she said unemotionally. It was like she was numb and had no feelings. "What is going on with you, you should be mad or hurt, tell us what's wrong!" Josh demanded. "Nothing's wrong, I'm fine!" she responded. "There, I heard a little bit of anger, that's good!" Josh teased. She just rolled her eyes. "Oh, and there, she's expressing to me that I'm being stupid, that's a really good sign!" Josh then used his German doctor voice, "Und, tell me, young lady, about your relationship wit your fadder?" Bethany had to laugh at that. "Ah-ha, da patient is cured!" he said.

Church wasn't so bad after all, the new pastor and his Irish wife were pretty cool, and they were a lot younger than the one he remembered when he was there years ago. After having Jesus move into his heart, Josh was actually interested in hearing the sermon and he listened very intently. The pastor was funny and energetic as he spoke. He talked about some guy in the bible named Nehemiah, a man that helped build the wall in Jerusalem. When the pastor taught, Josh could picture the scene vividly in his mind because it was described so well. Plus Josh was really interested in history thanks to his 9th grade history teacher, Mrs. Atwood. She made the boring text come alive by using lots of visual props and hands on learning techniques. He thought she was the best teacher ever. This guy was like that, he really believes what the Bible says and he teaches it like it really happened. Josh caught himself several times thinking, "*I need to check into this more. I'd like to find out the history of Jerusalem and about these kings who allowed the rebuilding of the walls and the temple*". His imagination got away from him and he pictured the king in the story looking like President Ronald Reagan, saying in a loud voice, "Mr. Nehemiah, BUILD UP THIS WALL!"

After the service, Josh went up to the pastor and introduced himself. "Hello Pastor Dan, I'm Cami's son, Joshua." "Hi Josh, it's nice to have you here! I've heard a lot of good things about you," the pastor said as he thought to himself, "*here's a young man who wasn't nodding off during my sermon he actually sat up and listened!*" The two of them clicked right away. "I hear you're quite the ball player," the pastor said. "Oh, mom told you I play baseball?" Josh sounded pleasantly surprised to know that. "Yes she did, I'd like to watch you play sometime, if you don't mind," the Pastor said. "Well, I do have a game this afternoon, if you want to come out today. The team is planning to cook out after the game, you and your family are welcome to eat with us. I think my mom is making her famous potato salad!" Josh said. "That sounds great Joshua! I'll talk to my wife right now about it, it sounds like fun!" the Pastor said as he went to find his wife. Josh found himself seeking out the friendship of older men and he seemed to do it deliberately, maybe to get back at his dad or maybe because he missed him, he wasn't sure why. Something was missing in his life and he was trying to fill the void. He had a good relationship with his dad when he was younger. They went camping and fishing together and they played catch in the back yard. Derek did all of the things dads are supposed to do, until Josh was around eight years old, a third grader, that's when he remembered his dad getting busier with work and spending less and less time at home. He recalled thinking that his dad must be good at his job because they would always send him around the world to fix things. And now to find out that he had been thrown into some prison somewhere and there was no way of knowing how to find him made Josh feel helpless. Suddenly he had a thought invade his mind, "*What if he's dead, what if they killed him? They do some pretty brutal things to people over there*". He tried to shake that thought then he remembered that Uncle Bobby had said that he had good news, not bad. His dad had to be alive. Deep under the anger and disappointment, Josh knew he still loved his dad. He silently said a prayer for him.

The Pastor and his family did come to the game that day and they had a wonderful time. Josh played for a team on a small, local league, just a bunch of guys who loved the game. He was the second baseman so he always got a lot of action and when it was his turn at bat he didn't disappoint his fans, he hit a line drive right over the short stop which dropped to the ground before the outfielder could reach it. They won 5 to 4 in an exciting tie breaker. After the game, they all headed for the picnic area for the cookout. There was a playground nearby for the children so the Pastor sent his two children off to play while he and his wife Miriam talked to Josh and Cami. Bethany sat near Josh, texting all the while. Josh was really enjoying the conversation, Pastor Dan and Miriam acted so "normal" and they were funny too! The pastor had a lot of great stories and Miriam's Irish accent made everything she said sound fascinating and mysterious, or so Josh thought. They had a way of bringing Jesus into every subject, like he was a big part of everything they did, Josh liked that. He was beginning to understand from his dreams that Jesus should be involved in all the areas of his life, even in his baseball games. The Pastor must have read his mind. "Hey Josh, God gave you a special talent, you're a great ball player! We had fun watching you play today, thanks for inviting us!" he said as they prepared to leave. Josh thanked them for coming and helped them by carrying their sleepy son to the van. It was then that he decided that Pastor Dan would become his pastor, and he made a silent commitment to go to church every Sunday so that he could learn more about his new friends, Pastor Dan, Miriam, they're kids and Jesus.

"Do you realize that you are following my leading Joshua?" Josh heard the familiar voice in his mind say. *"I am? What do you mean Lord?"* he responded in his thoughts. *"That's the church I want you to attend. I have plans for you there."* Jesus answered. *"The prompting to go to church this morning came from me, and you obeyed my voice. I'm proud of you,"* the Spirit said. Joshua looked up at the bright blue sky and smiled as he put his hand over his heart. *"Thanks Jesus, I want you to know that I'll follow you anywhere!"* he said sincerely.

God knew that Josh's commitment would be broken and renewed many times in his life, yet he was pleased that Josh had begun his journey of faith and even though the road would be rocky and Josh would stumble and stray off course, he would always find his way back home.

8

The Bedroom

Josh was quiet on the way home. "What are you thinking about honey?" his mom asked. "Oh, I was just thinking about dad, I can't get rid of this anger I feel toward him!" he said. His mother felt the need to do what all moms do, help. "I've been learning about spiritual warfare in my Bible study group, I'm going to ask God to tear down the strongholds that Satan has built in your mind, okay?" she asked. Josh agreed to let her do that, though not fully understanding what she meant by "strongholds". She immediately pulled over into an empty parking lot, *"this must be serious"*, he thought. He had never heard her pray like that before; it sounded powerful! "Wow mom, you pray like you mean it!" he laughed. "You should hear some of the women in my Bible study group, Satan best not mess with them!" she laughed. "It's too bad your dad and Caleb weren't there to see your game today, they would have loved watching you play," she said, trying to lighten the mood. Josh smiled at her and said, "I wish they could meet Pastor Dan and his family, I think they'd like them, don't you?" He asked. "I'm sure they would, maybe someday? I'm glad to hear you talk about your dad like this Josh, we have to believe in him, he would never smuggle drugs; we know him better than that!" she said. "And remember, Uncle Bobby said he has good news!" She added.

Cami's hopes had been lifted and she felt like she was going to make it after all. Life had been hard on her for the past two years and many times she had felt overwhelmed by it all. Time and time again she had depended on God to help her through days of depression and worry. Sometimes she felt like a soldier, because life is a battle and at times she found herself surrounded by the enemy forces that were attacking her from every side. How she wished she had more faith, but God knew her heart and he was trying to show her that she had more than enough,.... she just had to pick up her sword and shield and use them. The Bible study class was helping her and she was learning to fight back using prayer and the power of Jesus' name.

"I'm so proud of you two!" she said as she gave Josh and Bethany a big hug. "Thank you again for coming to church with me today, you've made me so happy!" It was great to be back in sync with his mom. Josh felt better knowing that she cared enough about them that she would struggle to provide for them, but he still couldn't understand why she had lied to cover for his dad; did he really deserve her loyalty?

He kissed his mom and sister good night and started upstairs, then turned back to ask his mom something, "Do you have a Bible I can use? I want to look up that story the Pastor talked about today." "I sure do, wait here!" she was back in a flash with a bible in her hands. "I bought this just for you and I've been waiting for the perfect time to give it to you. Here, I even had your name printed on the cover!" she had a big smile on her face as she handed it to him. "Oh wow, thanks mom!" Josh was genuinely happy to have his very own Bible and he intended to read the whole thing. He smiled and ran up the stairs holding his Bible like he would a new born baby. He quickly got ready for bed, turned on the small lamp by his bed and began to leaf through the pages. Since Josh had met Jesus he had been eager to learn more about him. He knew that this book was all about God so that made it more than just any old book, it was God's word, the greatest book ever written, and it had just become his most valuable possession.

On the inside cover his mother had written this: "Dear Joshua, I am so pleased to give you this Bible. Read it every day and let the words in it comfort you and inspire you to become more like Jesus."

He went to the index, found the book of Nehemiah and began reading it. It was very interesting, but he was getting sleepy and his eyelids kept closing. The harder he fought to stay awake the sleepier he became.

"Come with us Joshua!" he heard some people calling out to him. He was startled when a young woman grabbed him by the arm and said, "They are going to open the scroll and read it to us, let's hurry!" Joshua seemed dazed as he ran with her down a road made of smooth stones. "Where in the world am I now?" he wondered. "Could this be Jerusalem?" he asked out loud. The woman looked at him and rolled her eyes. Then she smiled and said. "Isn't it magnificent?!" They both looked up at the Temple in awe. Josh thought he heard violins and brass instruments playing music that touched his very soul, like the musical score of an epic movie. His mouth hung open at the sight of the Temple. "Wow, it's so beautiful!" he said quietly to himself. "We did it Joshua, the wall and the Temple are finally finished, and we are finally back where we belong!" she said to him with tears in her eyes. Joshua saw all of the people standing around the Temple looking up at it in wonder and amazement, each of them admiring it and the God for whom it was built. "Praise to our God! He is the one true God!" Shouts of joy were being yelled out one at a time.

Then they all shouted in unison, "Praise to God most high!" Josh knew they weren't speaking English, but he understood every word. Then from behind him, he heard some older people weeping sadly and saying, "Ah, but it's not as glorious as it once was! It's such a shame that the Temple Solomon built for God was destroyed by Nebuchadnezzar's army. Forgive us Yahweh, for we have sinned against you! Your Temple was destroyed because we would not obey your word." Other people were thanking God for bringing them back to the land that he given to them many years ago. As Joshua listened to the people around him, some rejoicing, some mourning, he began to understand what an important place this was to them. He felt honored to be standing with them but he also felt like an intruder, after all, he wasn't an Israelite and he didn't help them rebuild it. He looked up just as the leaders stood up at the blowing of a ram's horn. A big scroll was carefully opened and one of the men who looked much older than the rest stepped forward to read it, looking very distinguished in his long white beard, and blue robe, he began to read from the book of Genesis. Everyone stood in reverence to God, and the reading of his holy word, they hung on each word spoken by the priest.

He read the words with a loud, clear, and deeply masculine voice. No one moved a muscle, even the children were quietly listening to God's majestic word. It was then that Joshua felt something deep within him stirring; it was a feeling of being a part of something larger than life. Somehow he knew it meant that he was included in God's family and that he wasn't an outsider anymore, he belonged here as much as they did. He stood there and took in all of the sights and sounds. He could smell the sweet aroma coming from the Temple as smoke rose to the heavens and he could feel God's spirit in and around him, almost like a warm blanket wrapped around his shoulders. As the priest read on, Josh was slowly being enveloped in a thick fog, when it cleared, he was in his bed again. The crowd was gone and so was the Temple.

Josh was a little disappointed when he found himself back in his room after that experience. He sat there quietly for a long time almost afraid to spoil the feeling he was having, if he moved it might leave and he wanted to keep it as long as he could. But after a minute or two, his back began to itch. He tried not to move but he just had to scratch it! *"Oh well, it was nice while it lasted".* he thought as he turned off the light and got all comfy in his bed. He sprang back up suddenly when he thought he saw the shadow of someone standing near his bed. A cold, creepy sensation came over him and he shivered with fear, then he heard a low, raspy voice speak to him, "I don't know who you think came into your heart, but it wasn't God's son! You are still lost in your sins! God doesn't love you because you're too bad! You'll never be in his family!" "WHO IS THAT?" Josh yelled out. "YOU GET OUT OF MY ROOM! HELP ME JESUS. MAKE HIM LEAVE!" he cried out. After saying that, it got quiet and all he could hear was the dripping of the faucet in the bathroom. Then he heard a soft knock on the bedroom door. And with a squeak the door opened a little, Josh could see the Lord standing in the light. "You okay son?" Jesus asked. "I am now, who was that? Was it Satan?" Josh gasped. "Don't worry!" Jesus said. "But he told me that I'm still lost and that I'm not a part of your family!" Josh cried. "He lies! You do belong to me, don't believe his lies, believe what my word tells you and trust in me! Satan can only do what I allow him to do. I am with you always and I have appointed Gabe to be with you." Jesus assured him.

"Who is Gabe?" Josh asked. "Gabe is the angel who guards you. He is up on the roof right now." Jesus said, pointing up. "How long has he been guarding me?" Josh sounded surprised to find out that an angel was looking after him. "He's been with you all of your life, ever since you were born." Jesus said with a smile. "So sleep tight pilgrim, I'll be here whenever you need me." Josh thought Jesus sounded just like John Wayne when he said that.

Feeling safe and secure, he fluffed his pillow, pulled up his covers and went back to sleep.

Jesus entered Josh's room and found him fast asleep. He lifted his eyes toward Heaven and began to pray to the Father for Josh. Jesus, the Lamb of God is also the Highest High Priest who intercedes for his children, he prays for us. That night he thanked the Father for Joshua and he asked that he would be aware of Satan's lies and he asked that Joshua would have wisdom and understanding so that he would be able to stand firm and grow in his new faith.

A loud ringing woke him up from his dream within a dream. *"Am I awake or am I dreaming?"* he wondered. RING! "Now what?!" he complained as he reached for his cell phone. "Hello" he said in a gruff voice. "Josh, this is Kyle's mom, he's in the emergency room. Could you come down here?" she cried. "WHAT, what happened!?" he asked as he sat up in the bed trying to clear his mind and fully wake up. He pinched himself to make sure it wasn't a bad dream. "He was in the rodeo earlier tonight, riding a bull! After he was thrown off, the bull stepped on him! Please come now Josh!" she pleaded. "I'm on my way!" he said as he hopped into his jeans. "MOM, Kyle's hurt, I'm going to the hospital!" he yelled as he ran out the door.

While driving, Josh's mind flashed back to all of the times he and Kyle had played together as kids. He had so many good memories with him and even though they hadn't seen each other in a couple of months, their friendship was still as strong as ever, that's how it is with best friends, they have a bond that can't be broken. "God, please don't let Kyle die! Help him to be okay, please, God, I'm begging you!" he cried hard and he could barely see to drive. He drove up and down the rows of the parking lot searching for a spot, he found one, pulled his car in and put it in park. Glancing in the mirror, he rubbed his cheeks and dried his eyes before he got out and ran to the emergency room door.

"Josh, I'm glad you're here!" Josh turned toward the familiar deep voice. Frank grabbed Josh and gave him a big hug, he had been crying. Josh had never seen this side of Frank, he had always come across as a real tough guy and he looked like one of the "Hells Angels" when in reality, he was more of a "Wild Hogs" kind of guy. "How is he?" Josh asked. "He's in intensive care….I think it's bad!" Frank said as he broke down again. "I tried to talk him out of riding that STUPID BULL!" he said angrily. "Can I see him?" Josh quietly asked. "Come with me." Frank said as he led the way. Josh felt like a small fishing boat following in the wake of a huge battleship. Josh was tall but Frank was six and half feet tall with a large frame. He was wearing a sleeveless black shirt and vest, black jeans with a wallet chain and big black boots. His long hair was pulled back into a tail and his muscular arms were covered in tattoos. He had the biker uniform and attitude and he caught the attention of all the doctors and nurses as he swaggered past them. Josh had long wondered how his dad and Frank had become friends, they were so different. Derek was a clean cut, average looking guy but Frank definitely wasn't an average looking guy. It was the same with the moms. Kyle's mom was really nice but she was kind of loud and bossy and she wore lots of flashy jewelry and dressed in all the latest fashions, most of which she found bargain shopping. Josh's mom was nice, but much quieter and she dressed like a mom, sweaters and jeans. She talked a lot too, she just wasn't as loud.

Maybe they all became friends because the kids became friends first. There was one for each of them, Caleb's friend was their son Vance or "VJ", Josh had Kyle, and Bethany had Danielle or "Danny". They were neighbors when the kids were small and it didn't take long before the two families were getting together on a regular basis. They even went on camping trips together and twice they went on vacation together. After a few years Frank and Tammy moved just outside of town to a small farm. They bought a couple of horses and Kyle quickly became an excellent rider. When he had turned sixteen, he entered his first rodeo at the county fair. Not long after mastering calf roping he tried his hand at bull riding. His parents thought he would grow out of it, but to their dismay, he loved riding the bulls.

It was a long walk past many doors, desks, nurses and doctors. The two of them stepped into the room where Kyle's mom Tammy was looking after her son. "We only allow two at a time in this room!" the nurse scolded as she stepped in to check on Kyle. Josh was intimidated by the stern nurse and turned to leave. Tammy told him that he could stay while she and her husband stepped out. He walked over to the bed and saw his friend all bandaged up with tubes poking out everywhere. Gently, he took Kyle's hand and squeezed it. "Hey buddy, I'm here…. can you hear me? I'm praying for you man, and God's going to help you, I know he will!" Josh stood there in the dim room looking at all of the machines that Kyle was hooked up to. "Looks like you just need a tune up, or maybe an oil change?" he kidded, trying to lighten his own mood. The only sounds were coming from the machines and the nurses talking down the hall. He turned his head and tried not to cry, "God, can you hear me? My friend needs help and I don't know what to do!" he whispered as he quietly sobbed.

He took a deep breath and wiped his eyes, hearing someone talking just outside the door. The voice sounded familiar so he peeked out to see who it was. "Kayla, what are you doing here?!" he asked, surprised to see her in the hall talking to Kyle's parents. "Hi Josh, do you know Kyle too?" she asked, equally surprised. "He's my best friend." he responded. "I know him from the rodeo, I ride in the barrel races, and we met a couple of months ago at another rodeo," she said. "You and Kyle…., did you date?" he asked nervously. "No, no, we're just friends, he was dating my friend Darcy for a while, that's how I got to know him," she explained. "I was there when Kyle was riding tonight. It was so scary to see him trampled by the bull, I hope he's gonna be alright!" she said.

The two of them walked down the hall to the waiting room so they could talk. "I didn't know you rode in rodeos! We have a lot to learn about each other, don't we?" he asked as he took her hand in his. "We sure do! Who knew you and Kyle were best friends!?" she laughed. They stayed and talked for a long time, occasionally checking with Kyle's parents on his progress. "Kayla, do you believe in God?" Josh asked. "Yes, why?" she asked. Josh looked down and said, "I don't want him to die, he looks so bad!" She held him while he cried. "Would you pray with me?" he asked. "Of course I will," she responded. Before they could pray, Tammy burst into the waiting room, "He's awake! He woke up! Thank God, he's going to be okay!" she cried as she hugged them both. Josh looked up toward Heaven with tears in his eyes and whispered, "Thank you!" They came back to Kyle's room to see him, but the nurse shooed them out after a couple of minutes. Josh and Kayla left the hospital laughing with relief as they walked to the parking lot arm in arm. The two of them sat in her car a talked for another hour. They told each other about their families but neither one had said anything about their dad. Josh's phone rang it was his mom asking about Kyle. He told her he would be home soon.

"So Josh, you told me about your mom and your brother and sister, are you going to tell me about your dad?" Kayla asked. He pretended not to hear her and said, "Wow, look at the time, I better get home! I've got a lot to do tomorrow, I mean today!" he said. "Yeah, it is pretty late, I mean early," she replied, looking at the time. They said a long goodbye and left. As Josh drove home he wondered what he was going to tell

Kayla about his dad. Now he knew why his mom had lied about him, it was so humiliating!

He tried to be quiet when he came in the back door, but his mom was awake and waiting for him in the kitchen. "Oh Josh I'm so sorry about Kyle! I'll go to see him today. So he's pretty bad?" she asked. "He's going to be alright but he's really banged up! You can see the hoof print on his chest where the bull stepped on him, it cracked one of his ribs, and he has a big gash on his head from the fall," he said. Cami hugged him and said, "Just thank God he's alive, he could have died!" "Mom, would you call Pastor Dan later and ask if he would come up to the hospital to pray for Kyle? I've prayed a lot, but I want to call in the "Big Guns!" he said.

She laughed, "Josh, I don't think you realize it but your prayers are the "Big Guns" too!" "I know, I know, but I want to bombard Heaven with prayer!" They both laughed. "Sounds like we're in a war!" she said. "We are, the enemy has attacked Kyle, and we are calling for the troops of Heaven to counter attack!" he said. "Yeah, we've got them surrounded!" she laughed. Josh suddenly felt a little silly talking about prayer with his mom, *"It isn't cool to be Christian and it sure isn't cool to be hanging out with my mom discussing prayer!"* he thought. "Now you get up to bed and get some sleep!" she said as she pulled his head down to her level and kissed his cheek. He had no trouble falling asleep, especially since Kyle was doing better.

9

───❦───

The Bathroom

While Josh was in a deep sleep, he started dreaming about his "dream house" again. This time he was in the bathroom, sitting on the edge of a bathtub. He heard a light knock on the door, it was Jesus. "Do you know the purpose of this room?" he asked. Josh laughed, "Ah, yeah, I think I know what to do in here," he said, opening the door to let Jesus in. "It's different here, this is where you do your daily cleansing..." he said, Josh interrupted, "I know, I know, you don't need to explain...." "No, you don't understand, it's for spiritual cleansing, you need to wash your mind in the water of my word," Jesus explained. "Okay, that sounds really weird, what do you mean spiritual cleansing? How can I wash my mind....in the word?" Josh said, looking confused. "I've forgiven you of all your sin, but you will continue to sin. Each time you do, you'll hear my voice whispering in your ear, warning you to stop sinning, confess it to me and turn away from it; that means repent. You need to listen to me and stop right away, because if continue to sin and do it deliberately, you'll grow weak and cold spiritually. If you don't listen to my warnings, which will progressively get louder and louder, you will grow spiritually dull, and you'll eventually tune me out. And if you ignore my warnings long enough, your conscience will be seared, it will be so hard, the only way for me to reach you, will be to break you," Jesus explained, "and I don't want to have to do that to you." "How do I wash in the word, what does that mean?" Josh asked. "I'm going to leave the room now so you can take a shower or bath in this "special" bath tub. You'll understand what I'm talking about when you're in there," Jesus explained.

He left the bathroom and closed the door behind him giving Josh some private time, as he sat on the edge of the tub he began to see a clear image in his mind of a sin he had committed earlier, he had told a lie. Knowing it was God reminding him about it, he decided he better take a bath in the word, he was anxious to try it out anyway. He hadn't had a bubble bath since he was a kid; he poured some soap into the tub and turned on the faucet. As soon as he turned it on he heard a voice, "Thy Word is a lamp unto my feet," he turned the faucet off and the voice stopped talking. "Who said that?" he asked looking around the room. When no one answered, he turned the faucet back on. "The Word of the Lord is true...." the voice said. Josh shut it off again. "Who is that?" he asked. Again no one answered, so he continued to fill the tub and as the water ran the mysterious voice quoted bible verses. "In the beginning was the Word and the Word was with God and the Word was God........"

Jesus leaned on the wall just outside of the bathroom. He cupped his hands around his mouth and quoted the verses out loud, after all, he was "The Word." Then he quoted verses about lying, "Proverbs 19:5, "A false witness will not go unpunished, and he who lies will not go free. Proverbs 23:23, "Buy the truth and do not sell it; get wisdom, discipline and understanding."

Josh heard where the voice was coming from, he walked over to the door and said, "I'm sorry I lied, will you forgive me?" Jesus smiled, "of course, now go soak in the Word for a while, let it do what was meant to do, transform you," he said through the door.

When the tub was full, Josh got in and waited for something to happen, something did happen, he looked down and saw that he was fully dressed, in camouflage! *"WHAT! Why am I dressed like this, is this the transformation he was talking about?" he thought.* "BOOM, the door burst open! "GET OUUUUT!" shouted a large man who looked exactly like Arnold Schwarzenegger. He was also wearing camouflage, even on his face! Talking with a heavy Austrian accent he grabbed Josh by the jacket and pulled him out of the tub dripping wet and held him up in the air with his face close to his and yelled, "WHAT DO YOU THINK YOU AHR DOING?! YOU NEED TO BE COVERED IN MUD, THE ENEMY WILL SEE YOU! YOU AHR GOING TO GET US ALL KILLED!" Josh flinched when the man pulled back his arm and made a huge fist. "Oh, quit being such a baby! Now take your weapons and let's get going!" the man said as he tossed Josh aside and stormed out of the bathroom. Josh peeked out of the bathroom and looked in both directions. "What the heck was that all about?!" he said out loud. "That was a form of temptation," Jesus said as he walked toward the bathroom. "Temptation, are you kidding? Temptation doesn't look like that!" Josh said, shaking his head. "He's tempting you to follow him and he wants you to believe that only wimps and weaklings follow me. A lot of men think it's weird to love me, they think they're too tough and masculine to go to church, they'd rather stay home and watch football," Jesus said. That got Josh mad and he defended Jesus by saying, "You're no sissy Jesus, I know some paintings make you look that way, but you're not like that at all! You took a beating and you willingly hung on the cross, I know, I saw the movie! I'd like to see anyone else do what you did!" he huffed in aggravation.

Then he heard the big man yelling from down the hall, "DON'T BE A LITTLE GIRLY MAN JOSH! Pick up your rifle and GET OUT HERE!" Josh stuck his head out of the door and yelled back, "YOU CAN'T MAKE ME FOLLOW YOU! AND I'M NO GIRLY MAN!" "YOU AHR A DISGRACE TO YOUR UNYFORM!" the man yelled. Josh felt a little uncomfortable hearing that. "Well, what do you think Jesus, did I resist the temptation alright?" he asked. Jesus put on his sunglasses, turned toward Josh and said, "HE'LL BE BACK."

The scene faded. Josh jumped a little when he suddenly found himself standing between the pews of a church. Everyone around him was singing and clapping. Then from the back of the church came a loud noise. "BOOM" The doors flew open. The whole congregation stopped singing and turned toward the noise, it was him again, the commando, or someone who looked just like him. This guy was dressed in a long open coat, he had sunglasses on, of course, and he was carrying a large shotgun. The pastor of the church called out, "who are you?" The big man strode to the front, turned to face the people and said, "I'm da Pahty Poopa!" Then he calmly shot out all of the windows. After that the commando ran into the room and shouted, "I WANT ALL OF YOU MEN TO FOLLOW ME, NOW! Several of the men got up and stood by him. One man politely asked to get a drink and use the bathroom first. "THERE IS NO WATER! THERE IS NO BATHROOM!" the commando shouted. "But sir....I need to change first, I'm not dressed for combat!" the man said. "STOP WHINING AND GET OVER HERE! WE NEED TO BUILD BRIDGES AND STUFF SO WE CAN BLOW THEM UP! THE REST OF YOU CAN STAY HERE WITH YOUR MOMMIES!"

Josh just stood there wide eyed watching as the two big men had everyone cowering in fear. Then in walked Jesus. "Josh, take charge of this situation, I give you the authority!" he said. Josh leaned over toward him and whispered, "Do you see the size of that guy? His head weighs more than I do!" "Take a look at the patch on your arm, you outrank him!" Jesus said. Josh looked down at his patch, it read, "Child of God". He took a deep breath and stepped out into the aisle and yelled, "SARGENT FALL IN!" The big man lowered his weapon and stood at attention. "Your mission has changed, I want you and your men to remain here," he said, he enjoyed having the power to control the big guy. "But sir, this is a church!" the commando replied. "Exactly, and I want you to sit over there by your, "mommy!" Josh pointed and smiled. The man sidestepped into the pew next to the extremely large woman who was sitting alone in the second row.

She turned her head slowly toward him. Everyone gasped because she looked just like him except for the long hair, the exposed metal and wires on the side of her face and the red glowing light in her left eye. Even her voice sounded like his, only hers was robotic. "I AM A MODEL

T-800 I'VE BEEN PROGRAMED TO BE YOUR MOTHER," she said. Her hand jerked out and grabbed his arm, "SIT DOWN," she said. Her head turned stiffly toward the front, then she turned back to look at him again with her frightening face and said, "CLAP YOUR HANDS."

Jesus started to walk out then he turned back to say, "You did good Josh, now go back to your bathroom and this time, take a shower!" Josh was instantly in the bathroom. He was showered with some verses from second Corinthians, *"For though we live in the world, we do not wage war as the world does. The weapons we fight with are not the weapons of the world. On the contrary, they have divine power to demolish strongholds. We demolish arguments and every pretension that sits itself up against the knowledge of God, and we take captive every thought to make it obedient to Christ"*. Josh felt really clean after his shower, way down to his spirit. He dressed then looked in the mirror as he combed his hair and thought to himself. *"I'm good looking, I'm smart and I'm strong.... and I can defeat any temptation, no problemo!"*

Someone tapped on the door. "Who is it?" he asked. "Hey Joshy my boy, it's me, Pride, can I talk to you for a minute?" "Who…, what do you want?" Josh asked. I just wanted to tell you how great you are, but of course you already know that!" Pride spoke with a New York accent. "You da man, Josh, am I right or am I right?" he asked. "I don't know what you're talking about," Josh sounded confused. "Hey, forget about it, what, you think I'm not serious here?" said Pride. "I don't know you. I think you better leave, now!" Josh said. "You talking ta me? Hey tough guy, you talking ta me?! I will personally come in there and show you who I am, you want that, huh tough guy?" Pride taunted. *"This guy is weird, why is getting all mad?"* Josh thought.

He heard the tapping again, it was his mom outside his bedroom door. "LEAVE ME ALONE PRIDE!" he yelled. "Honey….. it's me, wake up! I just got another call from Uncle Bobby; he said he is at his dad's house in South Dakota. He'll be here later this week, he couldn't say exactly when, said he'll call me back soon," she said. Josh sat right up, still groggy from lack of sleep; he rubbed his face, smiled and said "That's great! I can't wait to see him and find out about dad!" He got out of bed, got dressed and went downstairs. His mom had breakfast waiting for him. After they ate, they drove to the hospital.

Pastor Dan was waiting for them when they arrived. "Hi Pastor, thanks for coming, I'll take you back to Kyle's room now." Josh said. As they walked toward the room they saw Frank approaching. "Hi ya Josh, hey Cami," he said, looking upset and tired, "Kyle had a bad night." "But I thought he was doing better?" Josh asked. "He was having trouble breathing, so they had to suction out his lungs." Frank explained. "Oh, I'm so sorry, is he breathing better now?" Cami asked. "He's has an oxygen mask on," he replied. "Frank, this is Pastor Dan, he wants to pray for Kyle, if that's okay with you?" she asked. "Of course, follow me." Frank led the way to the room in silence which was unusual for him. Tammy was standing near Kyle when they walked in the room. "Tammy, this is Pastor Dan, he's going to pray for Kyle," Frank said in his deep voice. The pastor greeted Tammy and asked if they would like to gather around Kyle's bed and hold hands. Tammy and Frank weren't church goers but they were willing to try anything at this point.

"Lord Jesus, we come together to pray for Kyle, we ask for a complete healing in his body. May there be no permanent damage to his lungs or ribs and we ask that his head injury would heal quickly. Keep him in the palm of your hand Lord Jesus, you are the one who made him and you are the one who can make him well again. Guide the doctors as they care for him and give them wisdom in what to do for him. We ask that he'll regain his strength soon. Please give his parents peace and may they have faith to trust in you Lord. I ask all this in the mighty name of Jesus. Amen." "AMEN" they all said. "It was so nice of you to do this for us, thank you Pastor Dan!" Tammy said. "I'll check on him again soon," he promised. Before he left the room, he turned to look at Kyle. "Look everyone, he's waking up!" He laughed. "Praise God!" they all cried.

They gather around his bed, he opened his eyes and smiled at everyone. Tammy leaned over and kissed his forehead, "You're going to be okay baby!" she assured him. The nurse came in to check on him. Everyone knew the drill; they moved outside and waited for her to let them know. "He's doing better!" she said as she walked out of the room. "The doctor is on his way. If everything checks out, Kyle will be taken off of the respirator today!" she said. "And he may be going home sooner than you think!" She was really nice and they liked her much better than the other nurse they had encountered. They all went back in to say good bye to Kyle, then they left so he could get some sleep. Tammy and Frank thanked Pastor Dan for his prayers. He was happy to have met them and he hoped to stay in contact with them, he had already promised them a second visit. His main goal was to introduce them to Jesus, the Savior, the one who actually healed Kyle, his second priority was to become a friend to them and show them God's love and the third was to disciple them and teach them God's word; but that would only happen if they we're open to it, so he began praying that they would be. Pastor Dan and his wife were the "real deal", they were striving to be as much like Jesus as they possibly could be, they had trials and they made mistakes, just like everyone else, but they kept on trying, and they never gave up.

10

---oଞ୧o---

The Medicine Chest

Cami picked up some lunch for Josh then dropped him off at home while she went shopping. While eating the food he grabbed the remote, turned on the television and flipped through the channels until he saw something he liked. He found an old program that had always made him laugh and he was in the mood for a good laugh. Watching a couple of episodes of the Three Stooges did the trick, he loved watching those guys! After that he began to feel the need for sleep since he hadn't slept much the night before. He went to the closet and found a pillow and blanket, then crashed on the couch, he was sound asleep within minutes.

In his dream he found himself lying face down on the hot ground. He sat up and spit out a mouthful of dry, nasty tasting sand, he had to rub his tongue with his shirt sleeve to get it all off. "Here, have a drink," someone said. A very pretty girl with long dark hair and big brown eyes handed him a strange looking canteen. She sat above him on a large rock. "Thanks!" he said as he filled his mouth with the warm water and spat out the rest of the sand that was in his mouth. "Where am I?" he asked standing up to look around. "Silly, we just came through the sea!" the girl said as she pointed to the beautiful blue water. Josh put two and two together, "I'm here with Moses and the Israelites aren't I? Where is he?" he asked. "Who are you looking for?" she asked. "Moses, you know, the big M, the burning bush guy!" he said. She looked at Josh like he was from another planet. "Moses and the people are on the other side of that hill," she said pointing to the east.

"Why are they already leaving this place so soon? I want to stay longer!" she said as she crossed her arms and pouted. Josh liked her accent and smiled at her as she went on and on. "I would like to sit on this rock and think about what just happened. Oh sure, we danced and we sang for a while, we thanked God for what he did, but then they all wanted to move on! Well, I'm not ready to leave this place yet Joshua! God did something wonderful, and I want to sit here and soak it all in. Why are they in such a hurry, I don't understand! God deserves our praise for what he did for us. Pharaoh and his army are on the bottom of that sea!" she said loudly, standing up on the rock and pointing toward the calm water that was split open only a few hours earlier. She was totally in awe of what had happened and Josh could tell that she was different from the others.

"I understand how you feel. I think God is super awesome, and he does the most amazing things!" he said, using his arms for added effect. "That's true, water is not supposed to do that, it was truly a miracle! I am glad you agree with me Joshua, we should be thanking him more, I want to tell him how much it means to me to be free!" she also used her hands and arms to add a punch to her words. "We are free from slavery, free to do as we please, that is a huge thing for me! No more breaking my nails lifting heavy bricks, no more mud squishing between my toes, no more arrogant Egyptian girls calling me names! God did so many miracles in Egypt, the blood in the water, the frogs, the locust, the darkness, and the Passover! Someone should record it all so we will always remember!" she said with emotion.

"Oh, it'll be written down, God will make sure it is!" he assured her. She thought about it for a minute. "Maybe Moses will do it, he is a man of God and he hears the Almighty's voice, yes, you are right Joshua, God will not let us forget these things. He is a good God and he has done many wonderful things for us! He brought us out of Egypt and he will take us to the Promised Land, I have faith in him!" she said with confidence. With that all settled, she took Josh by the arm and said, "Come Joshua, let us follow the cloud to the mountain of the Lord." Josh liked her spirit. "What's your name?" he asked. "Oh Joshua, you kidder, you know my name is Hannah, why do you act this way? Tell me you didn't lose your memory so soon, you are a young man! But, can you still run like a young man? I will race you over the hill!" she laughed as she took off running.

They both ran until they reached the crest of the hill. Josh gasped at the sight of the crowd following Moses and the cloud pillar. "Wow, look at all of them! He said, still trying to catch his breath. "You are so silly Joshua! You act like this is all new to you. I don't understand you sometimes," she said. "Hannah, let's find Moses, alright?" Josh asked. "Sure, sure, we can walk with him and his sister Miriam, let's run to find them!" she said, as she ran off. "What's with all the running? Hey, wait for me!" he yelled. They ran past the crowds of people and found their way to the front. "There he is, come on!" she yelled. "Oh my gosh, Hannah, aren't you tired? You should be on the track team!" he said as he tried to catch up to her. Suddenly he saw Moses standing majestically on a rock, holding his staff in his right hand. Josh froze in his tracks and stared at him. "It's really him!" he said. *"Moses does look a lot like the guy in the movie, The Ten Commandments," he thought.*

He walked up to rock and said, "Hello, Mr. Moses, sir, I'm Joshua, it's a real honor to meet you, sir!" he said as he held out his trembling hand to Moses. Like Hannah, Moses also stared at Josh as if he were from another planet. "Where did you get those strange clothes young man? Come over here, I want to see your sandals." Moses said in a commanding way. "They're actually not sandals sir." Josh explained. "Where can I get a pair?" Moses asked as he bent down to admire the red, white and blue stripes on the side of Josh's high tops. "These look like they would fit me, may I try them on?" he asked. "Ah, sure, hang on a minute." Josh sat down in the sand and took his shoes off. "WHATS THE HOLD UP?" someone yelled. "I'm getting hot standing in this sun! I could be sitting under a shade tree, but no, Moses has to try on the boy's shoes!" Someone else called out. "You want to hurry it up there Moses, my feet hurt, not that anyone notices MY feet! God forbid that I should get new shoes! No, I have to wear the same old sandals day after day after day…." "Okay, okay, I heard you! Stop with the complaining already!" Moses yelled out. "It kind of spoils the greatness of this story, don't you think?" he whispered to Josh. "If you mean all of the complaining, yeah, it does. What a bunch of whiners!"

"Unlike you Josh, you never complain, do you?" Josh stood up and looked for the man who had just spoken to him. A bearded man wearing a hooded robe stepped forward, pulled back his hood and smiled at Josh. "JESUS! What are you doing here?" Josh said excitedly. "I've come to take you home." Jesus responded. "You're taking me to Heaven already?!" Josh gasped. "No Josh, relax! I'm taking you back to your house. Better get your shoes back from Moses before he decides to keep them!" Jesus laughed.

"My Lord, it is you!" Moses said, bowing at the feet of Jesus. Josh suddenly felt guilty that he hadn't bowed when Jesus came to him. "This is no mere man Joshua. This is El Shaddai, the Lord God Almighty! He is Adonai, the Lord and Master! He is the creator and savior of all mankind and he is worthy to be praised!" Moses said as he bowed down again.

Joshua looked at Jesus and fell to his knees along with Hannah who had been listening to everything Moses had just said.

"What are they doing, bowing to this man?" someone in the crowd said loudly. With that, the whole crowd of people began to murmur against Moses. Moses stood up, removed the shoes from his feet and handed them back to Josh. "These are nice shoes Joshua, but I don't need them. My God supplies all that I need. In him I live and move and have my being." he said while looking at Jesus. "It's all about him, my dear young man. You see, I am nothing without him. I did not deliver the people from the Egyptians, my Lord did that." Moses said reverently.

Josh's eyes were opening more and more and he was getting a better view of who his new friend Jesus really was. Jesus smiled at him and helped him to his feet. Josh felt the most incredible love coming from the Lord's eyes. He blinked and looked again and what he saw in those same eyes took his breath away, it was a flash of fire! Josh dropped to his knees again, shaking like a leaf, "he really is God Almighty!" he gasped, afraid to move. "He is your friend and he is God, never forget that young man." Moses said as he offered to help Josh to his feet.

Jesus held his hand out to Josh and said, "Come with me Josh, I want to show you something back in your heart." Suddenly they were alone and back in the bathroom of Josh's heart house. It took a minute for Josh to adjust to his surroundings, he was already missing Hannah and Moses, "Couldn't we stay with them a little longer? I have some questions for Moses," he asked. "We'll see them again, don't worry," Jesus promised. They were standing in the bathroom again. Jesus walked over to the mirror, "Open the medicine chest," he said. Josh opened it and saw bottles of medicine, some bandages and assorted first aid items. "This medicine chest is for your healing and to make you feel better when you are sick or injured." Josh was a little disappointed by it, he said, "That's nothing special Jesus I have one of these in my real house." "Take a closer look." Jesus said.

Josh took one of the bottles off the shelf and read the label. "Laughter, take multiple doses each day." "Open it and see what happens." Jesus said. When he opened it, he heard voices coming from the medicine chest and he watched in amazement as the mirror became a screen, it was like a television program. "That's Peter, James and Thomas." Jesus said as he pointed out his friends to Josh, "Watch this, this is great!" he laughed. Josh laughed too as they watched Peter stepping over a rock, losing his balance and falling backwards, and landing on top of James. They went sliding down the muddy river bank and knocked poor Thomas right into the river. "They're just like the Three Stooges!" Josh laughed, that was hilarious!

"You see Josh, laughter is like good medicine. It makes you feel good to laugh and it relieves the stress in your life. It's like a release valve that lets out the hot steam. Use this every day because I sure wouldn't want you to explode from all that pressure!" Jesus laughed.

"Josh looked at another bottle. "This one says "Giving," what will this one do for me?" he asked. "Well, try it sometime, giving to others, especially someone in need makes you feel great inside. Let me suggest giving a blanket to the homeless man you see walking around downtown or mow the yard for the elderly couple who live on the corner. Josh shook his head in agreement. "Or take Kyle a gift, he'd like that," Jesus said as he put his arm around Josh's shoulder, "any time you freely give to others, helping them when they need it, you are pleasing me because I want you to be generous with what I have given to you," he said.

He reached up and took the box of bandages from the shelf. "Now this one is really special, read it," he said with a big smile on his face. Josh read the box, "Mom's hugs and kisses", what is this?" he asked. Jesus laughed and asked, "Tell me it doesn't make you feel better to have your mother take care of you? "Yeah, but I'm too old for that now," Josh said, pushing the box away. "You never outgrow the affection and love of your mother." Jesus said. "My mother was always there for me, even at the cross. It made it a little easier, knowing that she was there, and that she believed in me, no matter what. Love is the best medicine for a broken heart."

He put the box back, then he took a large clear bottle from the shelf, he opened it and out of the bottle a beautiful, translucent rainbow appeared. "It's so beautiful, what, what is it for?" Josh asked as he tried to touch the colored, airy bow. "This represents all of my promises to you, to all of you." Jesus said as he stood in the rainbow, "I will never leave you or forsake you," and, "The Lord is faithful to all his promises and loving toward all he has made. Psalm 145:13," he said. Then he lifted his arms, closed his eyes and smiled as spoke again, "I (he) will wipe every tear from their eyes. There will be no more death or mourning or crying or pain, for the old order of things has passed away. Revelation 21:4"

Josh woke up after that. "Wow!" he whispered. He lay motionless for a long time just thinking about the two amazing dreams he had just experienced, especially the one about Moses. When he finally sat up, he glanced over at his new shoes and laughed out loud thinking about how Moses had looked wearing them. "I guess I'll keep them after all," he said as he smiled and looked up, "Thank you Adonai, that was incredible!

11

The Armor Closet

Josh had to work later but he wanted to go by the hospital and check on Kyle first. He remembered what Jesus had said in his dream about taking Kyle a gift but he couldn't think of anything to give to him. "Got any ideas Jesus?" he asked out loud. Then a thought came to him, he didn't know if it was his idea or God's, he was pretty good at drawing so he thought he would make a large cartoon drawing of a bull. The bull would be holding a sign that read, "WARNING Bull riding may be hazardous to your health!" After he finished the drawing, he stood back, to examine his artwork, it was really colorful and creative, *"I hope this makes him laugh,"* he thought.

Kyle was awake and having some breakfast when Josh walked into his room. "Hey, you're eating, that's great! How are you feeling?" Josh asked. "I feel a whole lot better today than I did yesterday! Hey, have you seen my hoof print?" Kyle asked as he pulled the hospital gown to the side in order to show off the red mark on his chest. "Yeah, it's very impressive!" Josh laughed. "Yeah, it's going to leave a cool scar!" Kyle said proudly, smiling at his new trophy. "I made something for you," Josh said as he held up the poster. "Hah, hah, that's funny, I love it!" Kyle laughed. "I can still get you on my baseball team if you want," Josh asked. "Thanks, but I'll stick to riding bulls, baseball is way too dangerous!" Kyle kidded." Josh didn't really understand why Kyle enjoyed doing something so dangerous, but then again, he enjoyed some pretty dangerous things too, like mountain biking and white water kayaking. The two of them talked and laughed about some of the crazy and funny things that they did when they were kids.

"Glad you're okay, we were all freaking out, thinking you were gonna die!" Josh said. "Me too, it was kind of scary! Hey, what's this I hear about you going to church last Sunday?" Kyle asked. "Yeah, can you believe it?" Josh laughed. "You know something Josh, when I was lying out there on the ground and the bull's hoof came down on my chest, I thought about God," Kyle said. "I bet you did!" Josh laughed. Kyle got serious, "Do you think he's real, I mean God, does he really exist?" he asked. "It's funny you ask, I do believe he's real, I wanted to talk to you about it, I know it sounds strange, but I think I met him in my dreams, Jesus I mean," Josh suddenly felt uncomfortable admitting that he believed in God. He and Kyle had always made fun of Christians because they acted so weird, except for his mom, well, sometimes she acted weird too. She made them laugh whenever she'd talk about miracles and the Holy Spirit and stuff like that. They knew it hurt her feelings but they couldn't help themselves from teasing her, sometimes making her laugh too. And whenever she'd warn them about Satan and Hell, they would roll on the floor laughing, never taking her seriously. That reaction always made her mad, which also made them howl with laughter because she was really funny when she got mad.

"I'd like to hear about that." Kyle said. Something or someone had touched his heart because he started to get choked up a little and he had tears in his eyes. "Don't cry man! You're going to make me cry, and I don't cry!" Josh said. They both laughed. Kyle changed the subject. "Hey Josh, the girl that brought me this tray is really nice looking!" "Guess you are feeling better!" Josh laughed. "Quiet, here she comes!" Kyle whispered. "Hi there, are you finished with your tray?" she asked nicely. "Yes I am, and I ate every bit of it....Dakota," he said as he read her name tag. "Are you coming back later with my dinner?" he asked. "Yes, I'll be back with your meal, I work until 6:00 today, so I'll be back around 5:00," she answered sweetly. "Sweet, I mean, that's great!" he said. As she was leaving, she turned and smiled at him. "Um, Kyle, this is going to sound strange coming from me, but when you start dating her, because I know you will, try to be respectful of her, okay?" Josh asked. "Well, now I'm offended! You think I'm not respectful?" Kyle faked being hurt.

"The minute you see a cute girl, you flirt with her; it's like a challenge to you, then you'll date her for a while until another one comes along," Josh said. "Okay mom, I'll be respectful!" Kyle kidded. "Cut it out, I'm serious!" Josh said sternly.

"This Jesus has gotten into your head hasn't he?" Kyle asked. "*More like my heart.*" Josh thought. "Well, I'm no angel, but you haven't exactly been one either!" Kyle said smugly. "I know how bad I've been in the past, but I'm different now!" Josh explained. "Yeah, right, I don't believe that for a minute!" Kyle laughed. "I just think you should treat her, you know, like a lady, and make her feel special, that's all." Josh blushed to think that he did sound just like his mother. "I care about you and I want the best for you," he added and then immediately regretted saying it. Kyle stared blankly at Josh and then in an angry tone he said, "Who are you, and what have you done with Josh?" Then they both burst out laughing. "Oh man, that was funny!" Kyle laughed, "I care about you and I want the best for you!" he repeated in a high pitched voice. Josh laughed so hard he turned red. "Oh-man, don't you tell my mom that I'm turning into her!" "STOP, it hurts to laugh!" Kyle said holding his ribs, laughing and crying at the same time, "ouch, ouch, ouch!" he cried.

Josh left the hospital smiling because he had made Kyle laugh but at the same time he was feeling kind of dumb for saying those things to him. He wanted to be cool, but he was feeling differently inside now, he was becoming hyper aware of what was right and what was wrong as the voice whispering in his ear was hard to block out. Then he heard it again, it said, "*That was good Joshua, I'm proud of you! Kyle needs to know the truth, he needs to know me. I want you to talk to him again, soon, because he's ready to listen.*"

When he got to work, he put on his cowboy hat and bandana then he grabbed a wet towel and began wiping down the counter. He liked his job and he did it well. His boss, Joe, watched from a distance and was pleased that he didn't have to tell him what to do every minute. Josh saw what needed to be done and he did it. Joe was also happy with the way he treated the customers, he noticed him crawling under a booth to retrieve a baby bottle. He walked to the table and handed it to the young mother. Joe overheard their conversation, "Your baby has a good arm!" Josh laughed. "Yeah, I think he'll be a pitcher some day!" the proud daddy answered. Josh was taught to earn his money and to never waste time while on the job. Joe made a mental note of all the things he saw him doing, he was very impressed with his work ethic.

Josh finished work at 8:00. He drove home, got a snack and fell asleep on the couch watching television. In his dream, he was sitting in the kitchen sipping on overly sweetened coffee, just the way he liked it. "Good morning Joshua!" Jesus said loudly as he entered the room. Josh sprayed a mouthful of coffee across the table, "Good morning, cough, cough," he said. "Let me fix you some breakfast my boy, then I have something to show you upstairs," Jesus said in a cheerful tone. "Okay, sounds good, cough, cough." They finished their eggs and toast and then sat the dishes in the sink. "Come with me Joshua," Jesus said as he headed up the stairs.

At the top of the stairs Jesus stopped, turned to Josh and said with a flourish, "Prepare to be amazed!" He flung open the closet door and said, "Behold your armor!" Josh gasped as he saw the gleaming pieces of armor, but what really caught his attention was what opened up behind the shelves, it looked to him like the inside of an old castle. He ran into the immense room and spun around yelling with an echo, "It's huge in here, in here, in here!" He couldn't believe his eyes. "How did this castle get in my heart? This is awesome!" he yelled.

"This is where you will train for battle," Jesus told him. "I get to sword fight, that's fantastic!" Josh said. "Aye, Jesus said in his best Scottish brogue, you wull larn ta fight the forces of evil and wickedness, you wull!" He sounded just like Braveheart now. "Here is your sword lad, be careful, it has a double edge and it's extremely sharp!" He handed him a heavy iron sword. "Oh cool, this is going to be fun!" Josh swung the big sword around pretending he was in a real life sword fight. "It's not for fighting flesh and blood, it's for spiritual battle." Jesus explained. "Spiritual, what do you mean?" Josh sounded disappointed. "Ahh, laddie, the battlefield is in your mind, Satan has built up strongholds and fortresses in there" Jesus pointed to Josh's head. "Pray and I will destroy them all for you! Then you'll need to go in and take every thought captive and make them obey me," he added. "You mean like prisoners of war?" Josh asked. "Your thoughts may be hostile and unruly, but we can change them. They will become a mighty force for good, if we train them properly." Jesus explained. "Sounds serious, how do I do that?" "Yooz the wurd, it's powerful enough to defeat all of Satan's lies. He wants to kill, steal from you and destroy you lad, thus sword will scare him off; he hates it!" "Do you mean I can use bible verses against Satan and his gang of fallen angels?" Josh asked. "Aye, even a wee lass can chase him off with my wurd!" Jesus laughed. "But I don't know many Bible verses." Josh said. "Well, that is something we'll remedy won't we?" Jesus said. "Larn to yooz thus", he tapped Josh on the forehead, "then, I'll teach you to yooz thus," he tapped the sword. Josh smiled and asked, "Did you watch "Braveheart?" "Aye, I did." Jesus said. "Cool." Josh laughed.

"FREEDOM!!!!" Jesus yelled.

The loud yell woke Josh up. He laughed to himself and thought, "*You sure surprised me with that one!*" He glanced at the clock, "*seven thirty, I need to get ready!*" He and Kayla were meeting by the lake again at 8:00 to go kayaking. He quickly changed and drove to meet her. She was sitting in her car, talking on her phone when he drove up. They walked down the path until they reached the boat rental shop where Josh rented two kayaks for them, one red one blue. They headed out toward the middle of the lake. It was a warm morning and the sky was a beautiful bright blue. When they reached the middle of the large lake they stopped paddling, Josh reached over and took Kayla by the hand and they drifted as the soft, warm breeze gently moved them along.

"You know Josh, I'm a good girl," Kayla said teasingly, "and if you try anything with me mister, I'll sic my cousin Haylee on you, she's a black belt!" "Okay, okay, you're safe with me, I wouldn't want to get her mad at me, she sounds dangerous!" they both laughed. "Is she really a black belt?" he asked. "Yeah, you should come with me next week, I'm going to watch her spar, or fight, or whatever they call it," she said. "Sure, that would be fun, and besides that, I need to get on her good side, I wouldn't want to get beat up by a girl!" he kidded. They stayed on the lake for over two hours just enjoying the view and the conversation. "Are you ready to go eat?" Josh asked. "I'm starving, I didn't have breakfast!" she said, "I'll race you to the shore!" she yelled as she got a good head start. "*I wonder why all the girls I've met lately want to race with me?*" he thought as he tried to catch her. "*I better not tell her about Hannah and the other people in my dreams, she might not believe me,*" he thought.

They decided to have breakfast at a little place that was on the other side of the lake. It was nice on the outdoor patio where they sat, the view was so beautiful, the trees were in bloom with pink and white flowers and the sailboats were bobbing up and down in the shimmering blue water. Josh looked at Kayla and thought that she looked cute in her jean shorts and pink shirt with her long blond hair pulled up in a ponytail. She didn't dress like all the "cool" girls. Most of the time she wore jeans and cowgirl boots, and that was fine with him. He liked the fact that she was confident in who she was, she really didn't seem to care if the other girls teased her about her farm girl clothes. She looked back at him and said something that surprised him and made him laugh,

"You know Josh, I like your style, you don't dress like all the "cool" boys, and I'm glad, it's nice to be with someone who isn't trying to impress everyone. Besides, I hate the fads going around, I think they look ridiculous, don't you?" she asked, hoping she hadn't offended him. "That's so funny Kayla! I was just thinking the same thing about you!" he laughed. "And you're right about all the new fads, I think they're weird too! I don't know how those guys run with their pants that low?!" he said. "I know, right!" she answered. They went on to discuss religion. Josh felt comfortable talking to her about God, she didn't act like he was strange and she never laughed or made fun at what he had to say about it. "Have you ever heard of the armor of God?" he asked. "Yeah, a little bit, why?" she asked. "I had a dream about it earlier, it was pretty cool, Jesus said his word is like a sword and we can use it to defeat Satan attacks," he explained.

After eating and talking for another hour, they left the restaurant and walked along the wooded path near the lake. Suddenly out of nowhere, three teenaged boys surrounded them and began to shove both of them. They demanded money, which Josh gave to them, a whole fifteen dollars! But that wasn't enough for them, they seemed to be having fun making a fool of Josh and scaring Kayla. He was afraid of what they might do to her and he instinctively clenched both fists and readied himself to fight. When they moved in on her, he was beyond fear and moving into his protection mode. The boys used a lot of profanity and spoke like they were angry about something. They were very intimidating. Then the big guy spotted the ring on Josh's finger, he demanded that Josh take it off and give it to him.

It was the ring Josh had gotten from his grandpa and there was no way this creep was going to get it from him. The big kid pushed Josh to the ground then put his large hand on his cheek, holding him down. "If you don't take it off I'm going to hurt her!" the boy threatened. "Here, take it!" Josh said as he sat up and pulled off the ring. "Now leave us alone!" The big one laughed and said, "We want your car, give me your keys, NOW!" Josh stood up then he remembered what Jesus had said about his word being a weapon. He yelled the only verse that came to his mind, "GOD IS LOVE!" He kept yelling it over and over, "Jesus loves you guys. You don't have to do this, just leave and don't hurt her! God is watching you, so you better stop now!" he said with authority. One of the boys shoved Josh to the ground and then picked up a large stick to hit him with. He stopped short and stepped back as if something had startled him. Then all three of the boys turned quickly and ran off into the woods.

Shaking with fear and anger, Josh shook his head and whispered to himself, "It worked! Are you okay Kayla?" he asked. She stood there, half in shock. "That was so scary Josh!" she cried, "That was amazing, you made them leave us alone!" "Did you see the look on their faces?" he asked. "It must have been the Bible verse, remember, your dream?" she said. "I don't know Kayla… maybe it is true; maybe God's word is powerful?" he said. "I'm just glad that you did that Josh, thank you!" she said. "Thank God, he is the one who saved us, not me! Come on, let's get out of here!" he said grabbing her arm. On the way to the cars, they were silently holding on to each other thinking about what had happened and how bad it could have been. "I guess it's not safe to be out here at anymore," he said. "It's such a shame and it's not fair!" she complained. "No it isn't fair! We should be able to walk down here without being attacked!" he fumed.

"Should we call the police?" she asked. "Let's just get out of here!" he said as he walked her back to her car. "Next time, I'm going to fight back!" he said, feeling like a coward. "You did, you stood up to them Josh! There were three of them and they might have had a knife or a gun!" she said, trying to save his pride. "Yeah, that's true, but I would have taken them if they would have tried to hurt you, you know," he said. "I know you could have," she stood on her tip toes and kissed his cheek. "I'm proud of you. You're my knight in shining armor!" she said. He hugged her and turned his head toward the sky. He winked at God and said, "It is pretty good armor, isn't it?" Then he started to laugh. "What are you laughing about?" she asked. "Did you notice their pants? I guess they can run with their pants hanging low!"

12

The Storage Closet

Josh was really bothered by what had happened. After he said goodbye to Kayla he took a long drive so he could be alone and think. "I can't stand it, we were having such a good time and those jerks had to ruin it all! People like that make me sick! God, why do you allow bad people to run free like that?" he was ticked off. *"You did the right thing Joshua, you used the right verse and what you said made an impact on them, even if you don't care about them."* Josh heard the Spirit say. "God, did you just say that? It had to be you because I wouldn't have thought that way." It made him think, *"I wonder why those guys acted like that? I guess I wouldn't want them to end up in Hell, no matter how bad they are. If God can change me, he can change anyone!"* He decided that he should pray for them, "Jesus, you told me to love my enemies, well, those guys are my enemies, so please forgive them. I don't think they even realize how lost they are. Help them to see that they need you. Send someone to show them the way." Jesus smiled and sent a message into Josh's mind, *"I have the perfect person for the job!"*

When Josh got home, he told his mom about his date, but he left out the part about the three guys in the park. "I'd really like to meet Kayla, why don't you ask her to come over for dinner next week?" she asked. "I will, thanks mom!" he responded. That got her mind thinking way ahead to the wedding and to her future grandchildren. She smiled as she envisioned all of them swarming around her on Christmas morning, she saw herself smothering them with kisses. "Mom, mom, can you hear me? I'm going upstairs to bed, goodnight," he said. "Oh, goodnight honey, sleep well," she said as she came back to reality.

Josh kept thinking about Kayla and what had happened in the woods, "I don't want to think about those guys anymore!" he said to himself, but they kept invading his thoughts. He posted the pictures he took earlier of he and Kayla and read his messages. Then he tried to find something good on television but he was getting too sleepy to watch it. The struggle not to think about what happened earlier made him sit up and punch his pillow. "Okay God, what are you trying to tell me?" he whispered. "I want you to be the one who shows them the way." Jesus said. "Oh no, I prayed for those idiots, I mean those boys, that's enough! Besides, I don't think they're from around here, I'll probably never see them again," he said. No response came. "Why me, can't you send someone else?" he whined. It was silent in his room. "I must have imagined that," he told himself. He turned over and fell asleep.

"Joshua, come with me, I want to show you the storage closet, I cleaned and organized it for you," Jesus said as he opened the door. "This looks great Jesus!" Josh said as he checked out all things on the shelves. "Look, there's a big box of my memories, I'll look at that later," he said, not really interested in taking a stroll down memory lane. "What's this?" he saw a large black case labeled "MY DREAMS". "What's in here?" he asked. "Take a peek," Jesus said with a smile. Josh carefully opened the lid to the case and peeked inside, "it's a telescope," he said. "Set it up and aim it at that sky light," Jesus said, pointing up. Josh looked through the telescope and saw his dreams clearly. "Oh yeah, these are my dreams alright!" he said, adjusting the dial. "I can see myself; I own a go cart track, a giant arcade and a really cool miniature golf course, which I'll design myself! And that's me on the Coast Guard Search and Rescue team, cool! Whoa, that's me and Kyle dropping from a helicopter, we're skiing down a huge mountain, we're pretty good! I want to take a year and go on extreme adventures with him and my other friend Ryan. And there I am, I'm an archeologist, I'm traveling around the world digging up ancient ruins and treasure, this is awesome!" he said, turning to Jesus and giving him the thumbs up sign. He returned to the telescope, "This must be later in my life, looks like I'm about thirty and I've finally settled down. I live on a farm or a ranch near a big lake with a beautiful view of the mountains. This is great, I love this! I have horses and cattle and I grow corn, I can see it all so clearly! Looks like I have a big family, a big happy family! And yep, there's Kayla, she's my wife!" he said, pausing to look at Jesus. "All my sons go hunting and fishing with me, and my daughters are so beautiful and all of them are great cooks! We each drive a truck, a sports car, or SUV with a garage for each of them. Oh, and everyone in the family has their own four wheeler, motorcycle and jet ski." He turned to Jesus and said, "I may not be able to have all this stuff and do all of these things, I don't think that's very realistic, do you? I'll have to decide which dreams to go for but it's going to be hard because I like all of them."

"My, you do dream big!" Jesus laughed, "I like that! Why don't you look inside this case now?" he handed Josh a smaller black case labeled "God's Plan for My Life". Josh dreaded opening it, "Oh, okay, but knowing you, you're going to want me to be a missionary or worse, you'll want me to become a preacher!" he complained. "Just open it!" Jesus said. Josh opened the small case and inside he found what looked like a small telescope. He held it up to his eye and looked through it. "It's a kaleidoscope!" he said as he twisted it. "It's beautiful, but I can't make anything out, it's not clear to me. What does this mean?" he asked "It means, I want you to trust me with your life because I have good plans for you," Jesus said. "Do you want me to let you take over?" Josh asked. "We can't both be in the driver's seat, but you can ride shotgun!" Jesus laughed. "It may not make sense to you now, but if you let me, I will make something beautiful with your life," Josh let out a loud sigh, he didn't know how else to respond. He handed the case back to Jesus and changed the subject. "What's this?" he pulled a box off of the top shelf. It was made of gold and silver and the lid was decorated with colorful sparkling jewels. "Open it," Jesus said. Joshua carefully unlatched the box and slowly opened it. "I don't see anything." "Reach inside," Jesus said. Josh put his hand in the box. Then his whole arm went in as he felt for the bottom. Suddenly he jerked his arm out and threw the box across the room. "Ouch, that hurt!" he yelled as he examined his hand. Something slimy just bit me!" he yelled again.

"Yuck, that box is nasty inside and it stinks! What is this box?" he asked as he kicked the lid shut. "It's a box of lessons, life's lessons, each one is different." Jesus said handing the box back to Josh. "I don't want that thing!" Josh said, pushing it back. "You need it, you'll learn a lot from it," Jesus said, pushing the box back to Josh. "I don't need to learn anything from that box!" he said, pushing it back again. "If you don't use it, you'll have to learn you're lesson the hard way!" Jesus said. "You mean that wasn't the hard way?" Josh asked. "Why is it so beautiful on the outside and so disgusting and scary on the inside?" "Okay, I'll tell you, Jesus said looking at the box, "Sometimes bad things come in beautiful packages," then he reached for an old, dirty, cardboard box and handed it to Josh. "Open this one," he said. Joshua looked at Jesus then he carefully opened the box.

Inside was a black velvet cloth. He carefully held the cloth, trying not to drop what was inside. Between the folds of cloth he found a beautiful white pearl. "Don't judge by the package, Joshua." Jesus said. Josh thought about it and said, "You're right, I've done that with people, that's what you mean, right, I shouldn't judge people by the way they look?" "Yes, that's what I meant. I look inside everyone and I look for good and pure motives that come from their hearts. People can say and do anything to impress each other, but it's what's in their heart that matters to me," he explained. Joshua carefully set the pearl in the velvet cloth, folded it and placed it back in old box then he put it back on the shelf. He slid the beautiful box way back on the shelf and put some other boxes in front of it.

"What else do we have here?" he asked as he looked around. "This box of self- confidence is pretty big," he said as he tried to lift it off the second shelf. "Careful, you'll hurt your back!" Jesus warned. "Nah, I'm good!" Joshua said confidently. "You sure that's not a box full of arrogance?" Jesus kidded. Josh ignored the comment, "Hey, my baseball mitt, does this mean I'm good at sports?" he asked. "You are gifted in sports and art. I've given you many talents and abilities. The question is, how will you use them?" Jesus asked. Josh didn't seem too interested in answering the question. "I don't know yet, I've got lots of time to decide," he answered. He then saw a box that got him curious, "What is this, my insecurities, I'm not insecure, am I?" he asked taking the box off the shelf. "Everybody has some insecurities Josh, see what yours are," Jesus said. Josh opened the box and looked inside. It was full of colored folders. He grabbed a red one labeled "THE COOL FACTOR"; he opened it and started reading. "This says I am insecure about the way I dress," he said as he flipped through the pictures. "I've never felt like I'm cool, I'm no nerd, but I'm not cool either," he sighed. "I've tried to dress the way the other guys do, but I feel like an idiot and it's not comfortable to me." "Well, how do you feel about that now?" Jesus asked.

Josh thought for a moment and then he said, "Well, since Kayla told me that she likes the way I dress, I guess I'm alright. I feel free to be who I am and to dress the way I want. Does that mean that I can throw this folder away?" he asked. "I would," Jesus answered. "Good, I don't have to worry about that anymore!" Josh said as he tossed the file in the waste basket. Then he pulled out the blue folder and read the label. "MIDDLE MAN" "Oh, I know what this is. I've always felt that mom and dad like Caleb and Bethany more than they do me. I guess that's common, huh?" he asked. Jesus explained to Josh that they each were different but that they were all special to their parents, in their own unique way. "Your parents can't ever give you all the love and attention you crave, that's my job! Find fulfillment in me, after all, I am love!" he said. "You're right Jesus, my parents are only human, and I can't expect them to be everything I need, besides, I'm older now and to be honest, I'm over being jealous." he said, throwing the folder away without even asking if he could. "Let's do one more folder, okay Jesus?" he said pulling out the yellow folder. "Sure, we can go through as many as you want," Jesus said. "This one is marked GORILLA TOES! Aw man, you know how I feel about my toes!" Josh laughed. "Are you saying I did a bad job on your toes?" Jesus asked. "I don't know why you made them so hairy and curved? I feel like Big Foot!" Josh complained. "I made you the way I wanted you. Why, I can remember when you were a baby, your mother was always kissing your cute little toes!" Jesus laughed. "Well, they aren't so cute and little anymore! Okay, I guess I'll have to live with them, besides, they go great with my hairy legs!" Josh laughed as he got rid of the folder. It seemed as if Josh's storage closet was as big as a warehouse. He was having fun looking at all of the stuff in his life and although Jesus had cleaned out most of the junk, there were some things that Josh would need to take care of, he had some old problems, habits and attitudes that were going to be harder to let go of than his favorite pair of jeans.

Jesus pulled a couple of books off of the shelf and a pair of hiking boots. "Put these on Josh, they'll help protect you from snake bites." "What do you mean snake bites, where are you taking me?" Josh asked as he sat on a box and slipped on the boots. As he stood up he was surprised to find himself in the middle of a dense jungle. "Here take this machete and start clearing a path in that direction," Jesus said as he too began cutting through the thick plant life growing everywhere. They made a path to a steep rock cliff that overlooked a beautiful panoramic view of the valley below.

They stood next to a magnificent waterfall which was so close they could feel the cool spray from the water on their faces. "Step over here Josh and look through this window," Jesus said pointing to a free floating picture window. "*This doesn't make sense, how can this window be out here in the middle of nowhere?*" Josh thought. "What is this window doing here? What is it for?" he asked. "This was your view of the world before you knew me. Look through it and tell me what you see," Jesus said. Josh stepped close to the window to take a look and he was surprised at what he saw, "What a cool window, I can see everything from here!" "Describe it to me," Jesus said as he sat down in the grass, leaned against a tree, and picked up a fuzzy caterpillar that was crawling on the ground. "I've changed already. I don't see the world like this anymore!" Josh said. "Yes, your views are changing and the more you understand and learn about me the more clarity you'll have," Jesus said. Josh could see how he used to look at people. "Wow, I was pretty shallow and superficial, wasn't I?" he asked. He saw how he had judged people by how they looked on the outside. The view from the window revealed to him his thoughts and actions towards others. Most of the things he saw were good, some of them weren't very nice, and some were horrible.

Josh felt ashamed of himself for thinking that way. He glanced back through the window and pointed, "Look, that's me way down there? I remember that day, it was the first time I realized just how small and insignificant I was in the world." It was his first time in a big city. He was surrounded by huge sky scrapers and busy streets filled with traffic. There were thousands of people walking up and down the sidewalks, and they all seemed to be in a hurry. Back home he had always felt important, people knew his name and noticed him. But in that huge crowd he felt like he was invisible. After that experience he was afraid that a huge God would never notice a tiny speck like him. "It must have been kind of like "Horton hears a Who," Jesus said. "We are here! We are here!" he laughed. "Joshua, don't you know that I knit you together in your mother's womb? I know how many hairs are on your head, I've even written your name on the palm of my hand!" he said. Josh smiled and looked over at him as he played with the tiny caterpillar. He sighed with relief; it was such a great feeling to know that he was important to God after all. Then he laughed with delight when he saw Jesus instantly turn the caterpillar into a beautiful butterfly and release it into the sky. "This represents you." he said. They smiled at each other, "You are so amazing, I feel good when I'm with you," Josh said. Then he turned back to the window.

"What's that over there?" The window was zooming in on random people around the world. "It looks like some weird religious ritual, a bunch of men whipping themselves on the back until they bleed. What's that all about?" he asked. "The religions of the world are mankind's desperate attempt to work their way to Heaven or Nirvana or whatever they choose to call it. They either don't know or don't care that I took the punishment for them. All they would have to do is turn to me and ask me to forgive them. I would save them all if they would only ask," he said. "I love them all so much." Josh shook his head and said, "I used to be confused like that." He had heard that everyone would go to Heaven and that all faiths were equal and no one religion was better than another. His mother had told him otherwise, but he wasn't sure who to believe. "Some of my teachers said that there are no absolute truths, is that true?" He asked.

Jesus chuckled, "Really Josh?" He pointed his hands in opposite directions and said, "Left is one way and right is the other, isn't that true? 1+1=2, not 3, correct? You know there are set truths that will never ever change, only a fool would believe otherwise! I want you to know that you can always trust me, I AM the truth, all other religions are false," he said. Josh agreed. He turned back toward the window and saw three books, the Bible, Darwin's book on evolution, and a book about ancient aliens. "I wasn't sure if you were real, I wanted to believe in you, but I just didn't know for sure," he said, trying to explain that he had been searching for meaning in his life. Being an optimist, he had wanted to see life as happy, fun and fulfilling but it wasn't always like that. "There are a lot of bad things in this world," he said. "Tell me about it!" Jesus said as he walked over to the window and raised the clear rose colored shade. "It's good to see things as they are but it's also good to try and make a difference and bring love and light into a dark and sinful world."

He pulled out a bottle of his special window cleaner and a white cloth and began wiping the glass. "Now take another look, this is your world view now," he said. "Wow, what a change! I see people differently now, they're actually beautiful!" Josh said, excited by the view. "They look valuable, is this how you see them?" he asked. "Yes, each person is unique and special to me," Jesus said. "Oh, look over there," Josh pointed, "The Bible is getting bigger and it's blocking my view of the other books." "That's great Josh! Now let's make those two books disappear for good, follow me," Jesus said. Josh turned around, took two steps and suddenly found himself inside a large building full of airplanes and jets. He followed Jesus as they walked past a row of them, he whistled and said, "Look at these "bad boys", they're gigantic!" There were passenger jets, fighter jets and military cargo planes everywhere. Then they came upon what looked to be the parts and pieces of a large plane scattered all over the floor.

They stopped to look at it, then Jesus asked, "Now Josh, do you think if we wait a thousand years this jet will assemble itself?" "No way, that's never going to happen!" Josh responded. "Well, let's give it a million years, or ten million years, would that be long enough?" he asked. "These jets are way too complicated, it could never happen that way, someone has to assemble each piece. They all have to fit together perfectly to make it work, and you need every part working at the same time," Josh said. "That's right, it's impossible. Now, did you know that your body is much more complex than this jet? Even your tiniest cell has working parts, kind of like a miniature factory with a fleet of tiny trucks that pick up and deliver cargo. Charles (Darwin) never knew how intricate cells are and he didn't have a clue about your DNA. His theory can never be proven because it was made in ignorance of these things. Anyone who believes his theory is willfully ignoring the evidence of the design and function of everything. It was I alone who designed and created you and every other creature on earth". Jesus said.

"I placed all the systems in your body to work together perfectly; the skeletal, the respiratory, the digestive, the muscular, your circulatory system, the reproductive system, your glands and nerves, your brain and your skin. I could go on and on. You were put together with great care and planning," he said as he put his hand on Josh's shoulder. "I gave you the ability to think and reason and to feel love and joy. It was I who gave you all of your senses; taste, sight, smell, touch, and hearing. And most importantly, I gave you a spirit that will live forever!"

"Now let me talk about the Earth," he said. "Can you explain how it turns at a constant speed while hanging on nothing? Or do you know how it stays in its orbit around the sun? Everything about the earth is so precisely balanced and spaced that scientists say it's in the "Goldie Locks" zone, just right, it's precision tuned perfection! I could go into how water, air and plant life sustain life on Earth, but do I really need to say more?" he asked. "No, that settles it for me!" Josh laughed.

"Now about these aliens, well, it's a long story, come with me and I'll explain," Jesus said. He took Josh on a whirl wind tour of the places on the earth that some believe were made by ancient aliens, like the pyramids in Egypt and in South and central America, the sculptures on Easter Island, Stonehenge in England, the giant drawings in the desert and the giant monoliths in Peru. "Who made these things Lord? They're too huge for men to move, and these giant rocks fit together like a puzzle. There are so many mysteries in the world!" Josh said.

"After I created mankind and they multiplied on the earth, the fallen angels looked upon the women and desired them. They mated with them and their offspring became corrupted beings. Their very DNA was changed! They were called the Nephilim and they taught mankind all sorts of evil. Satan and his followers wanted to destroy my creation by changing it. It was his attempt to stop the messiah from being born. Both man and beast were tampered with until the whole world was corrupted and there were no longer any pure humans, except for Noah and his family. Noah's DNA was still perfect, the way I had made it. I sent the flood to destroy the work of the fallen ones not only because violence and evil had spread throughout the world but to save mankind whom I loved. Now Noah was also a righteous man who walked with me and obeyed me by building the ark, just as I had instructed him to. So I saved him, his family and a pair of every uncorrupted animal in the ark. Years later, the Nephilim were back on the earth, some of them were giants with great strength. They built huge structures all over the Earth and they made people believe that they, the Nephilim, were gods.

All across the world there are false religions and myths of gods and goddesses coming down to earth from the sky. Today many believe these "gods" were visitors from another planet. Satan will create a great deception in the last days and many people will believe in flying saucers and star people who can enter the world through star gates. He has been busy crafting this lie through books, movies and television programs and he is targeting your generation with this propaganda. Now, Satan is clever and he has the ability to create these great deceptions and he is planning to deceive the whole world with them. Many will even believe that I am from another world and that I am only one of many gods from outer space. It's quite an elaborate scheme, very convincing for those who don't know my word. Don't be fooled by him Josh, I am the only God, there are no others!" Jesus explained. Josh was wide eyed as he tried to process the information. "Satan is frantically trying to destroy the world because he knows his time is about to run out. And through the antichrist he will try to put "his mark" on everyone. I have warned the world about this many times. But you don't have to fear Joshua, my bride, the church, will be safe with me. I have already conquered Satan at the cross and in the end he and his followers will be cast into the lake of fire." Jesus said. Josh stayed quiet for a moment as he thought about what Jesus had told him. His thoughts were beginning to shift into a whole new paradigm, of truth.

Then he spoke, "Thanks for clearing that up for me Jesus. You love the world. It's Satan who hates it!" Josh was angry and disgusted with Satan for always trying to deceive and destroy people. "Go ahead Jesus, throw that garbage away!" he said without hesitation. Jesus stood on the cliff and flung the book about evolution and the one about ancient aliens into outer space. "Wow, you've got a good arm there!" he said. Jesus took out his extra, extra smart phone and showed Josh where to get more information. "This is my friend L.A. Marzulli" he said as he opened up L.A.'s blog. "He's been very instrumental in getting the message out about these things. While most of the church is asleep, or preoccupied in worldly pursuits, he's one of the few who are actively seeking out the truth and piecing together Satan's secret plans to deceive the world. Most of my people don't understand these things; they don't take the time to study my word and they will be deceived by the things that are coming, many will fall away from the truth and believe his lies. Show this to your friends Josh, teach them the truth and tell them about me," Jesus said. "Now I'm beginning to understand the Bible stories I've heard. I used to wonder why you had the Israelites go into the "promised land" and wipe everyone out, even the women and children, it wasn't because you were cruel… it was because they weren't human anymore. They were demonic creatures. When you plug the fallen angels and the Nephilim into the story, it all makes sense," he said.

The scene faded and they were back in the storage closet. They walked out and closed the door. Then Josh looked at Jesus and said, "I sure have a lot of stuff in my life! I'm a very complicated guy aren't I?" "There's much more to you than this handsome face!" Jesus kidded and patted Josh's cheek. "And if you think you have a lot of stuff, you should see inside a woman's closet!" he laughed.

13

The Treasure Room

"And I call this your "treasure room" although it's more of a closet than a room," Jesus said as he opened the door. They walked into the small room, the only thing that was in there was a safe. Jesus stooped down and turned the dial back and forth then he pulled the handle down and opened the heavy black door. Inside Josh saw the things he treasured most in his life, his family, a picture of Kayla, sports memorabilia, some cash, models of sports cars and a jeep, a picture of his dream house, and some brochures of places he'd like to visit someday. "Here, take this box out of here," Jesus handed him a box from the safe. Josh looked through the things in the box. There were toys, candy, a homemade sling shot, a rock collection, some baseball cards, and assorted things that he had treasured as a child. Now that he was nineteen, he had more mature treasures. *"It's funny how important these things were to me when I was a boy,"* he thought.

Jesus rummaged through Josh's treasures, "You know most of these things are earthly treasures, these material things won't last long. They'll all fade away or rust, but if you store up treasure in Heaven, it will last forever and no thief can ever steal it from you," he explained. "Well, how do I store treasure in Heaven?" Josh asked. "All the good things you do for me and for others will bring you a reward someday if you do them with the right motive," Jesus said. "What do you mean a right motive?" Josh asked. "Well, if you only do good things to get praised or promoted by others, it means nothing to me. Good things done out of love and concern for others or for me I consider to be a pure and good motive. If you give something just to get something in return, that will be your only reward, you'll forfeit your reward from me. Give in secret so no one sees. But remember, I see what you do in secret and I will reward you openly in front of everyone!" Jesus explained.

"Even a cold cup of water given in my name will mean you have earned treasure in Heaven," he said. "So I strongly encourage you to build up your treasure because I want to reward you! Just as any father loves to lavish his children with good gifts, so I love to give gifts to my children! But don't be a show off with what you have! If you are blessed with money or things, don't use it all for yourself and don't boast about it to make others envy you. Be a blessing to those in need, look for someone who has a need and help them. Do something kind every day. There are so many ways to give to others, even your time is something you can give. There are a lot of lonely people out there who would love it if you spent some time with them," he said. They closed the safe and headed downstairs. Josh felt like having something sweet to eat. "Want to go with me to the corner store for some ice cream or donuts or something?" he asked "You go and I'll catch up to you. There's a June bug in the back yard that needs my help in turning over," Jesus said. "Okay, that sounds kind of weird!" Josh said as he grabbed his wallet and ran out the door, "See you later!" He whistled as he walked down the sidewalk toward the store. On the way he passed an older woman in a motorized wheel chair. He said hello to her as he walked by. "Oh, hello, young man, can you help me with something?" the woman asked sweetly. He turned back, "Sure, what can I do for you ma'am?" he asked politely. "Both of my shoes came untied and I can't reach them. Would you tie them for me?" "Of course I'll tie them, no problem!" He said as he bent down to tie her shoes. They introduced themselves to each other, her name was Audrey.

"Oh thank you Joshua! Can I ask for one more favor?" "Sure, what else can I do for you?" he asked. "Well, I made a chocolate fudge cake and I need someone to try it out. It's a new recipe. Would you like to have a piece? I just live a block away," she said. "That sounds great! I was just on my way to the store to buy something sweet, then BINGO, you showed up offering me chocolate cake!" he laughed. "Do you like bingo? I like to play bingo!" she said. He walked beside her as she drove her scooter home. *"It's nice of you to go with her Joshua, she loves having company."* Jesus whispered. "Thanks Lord." Josh said out loud. "Oh, you're a Christian, I just knew it!" she said as she spun around to face him. Josh yelled out as Audrey's scooter turned and pushed him into the flower bushes. He struggled to get up and finally flipped himself backwards and landed on his feet. "I meant to do that!" he said as his face turned red. "I'm so sorry Joshua!" Audrey gasped, "Are you alright?" "I'm fine, I'm fine," he lied, she hurt his pride. As they continued on their way Jesus whispered in Josh's ear, *"You have to watch out for Audrey, she's not a very good driver!"* They both laughed at that. "Now I know what that June bug felt like!" he whispered back.

Josh had a really nice time with Audrey. She told him stories from her childhood and showed him pictures of her late husband, Phil, her four daughters and they're families. She reminded Josh of his own grandma. "Can you come back soon? I'll make you some homemade chicken and dumplings or biscuits and gravy!" she said trying to convince him to return. "I would love to! And the next time I come over, I'll fix that lose board on your porch?" he said. "Oh, you're such a doll!" she said as she waved good bye. "I'll see you next week Josh, don't forget!" "I won't, and thank you for the cake, it was delicious!" he called back. As he walked back home he heard Jesus say, *"That's treasure in Heaven my boy!"* "Really, I forgot about that!" Josh said excitedly. "If that's true of me, then Audrey will be rich in your Kingdom, right?" he asked. *"Oh she's earned treasure, big time!"* Jesus replied. *"But let's keep that our little secret, okay?"* he laughed.

Josh woke to the sound of the alarm and had to think hard to remember what day it was. He looked at his cell phone to find out. *"Wednesday, I'm losing track of time!* he thought. He jumped out of bed and took a quick shower then dressed for work. He had to be at work by

10:00. His mother offered to make him breakfast but he was in a hurry so he said no to her and went out to his car. His car wouldn't start! He tried several times but it just clicked when he turned the key. "Great, that's just great, I don't have time for this!" he complained. The back door slammed as he walked in and yelled, "Mom, can you take me to work, my car won't start!"

As they were pulling out of the driveway Josh noticed an old woman coming down the sidewalk. "STOP!" he yelled. "WHAT!" his mother yelled back. "It's Audrey!" he exclaimed. "Who's Audrey?" she asked. "It's Audrey from my dream, she's real! This is incredible!" he said excitedly.

He rolled his window down and yelled, "Hi Audrey, it's me Josh! Remember from the dream? I had cake at your house!" The woman looked confused but waved at him anyway. "Hello, do I know you?" she asked. "I'll be over next week to fix your porch!" he yelled out. "Okay, thank you, I think?" She waved good bye as they drove off. "Joshua, you scared her!" his mother scolded. "I probably did, but she really was in my dream! Oh, never mind, I'll tell you later," he said. Josh was amazed that Audrey was a real person and he kept shaking his head, "Can you believe that mom, she was in my dream!" he laughed. "You have to tell me all about these dreams tonight," she said as she stopped at a stop light. "Just drop me off here," he said. "But we're a block away!" she protested. "Exactly, he said. "But why?" she asked. "Mom, think about it, I don't want anyone to see me riding around in my mother's minivan, it's humiliating!" he said. "Thanks for the ride!" he said as he got out. "Oh brother, I wouldn't want to humiliate you in front of your friends!" she laughed and drove away.

Josh got to the restaurant a few minutes late. He grabbed his hat and bandana and headed for the front when he heard Joe yell, "Hey Josh, why are you late?" He didn't wait for an answer, "Get table 15 and 16 set up then take these dishes out back!" he barked. *Wow, Josh thought, what a jerk! I've never seen Joe act like that before,"* Josh thought. He grabbed a wet cloth and some silverware rolls and headed for the tables grumbling under his breath." *I should quit, I don't deserve to be yelled at. All the other employees come in late. This is my first time and Joe jumps all over me! That's it, I'm through here!"* he thought. Josh was building up steam like the boiler on a steam engine train. He finished the tables and pushed the cart of dirty dishes to the dishwasher to load them. He was as hot as the steaming hot dishwasher when he heard Joe say in a soft voice. "Hey son, I'm sorry I snapped at you like that." Joe looked really sad as he spoke which took the steam right out of Josh's engine. "Aw, that's okay, are you alright Joe?" Josh asked, feeling guilty for getting so mad at Joe. "Step into my office Josh," Joe said.

He asked Josh to sit down and he sat down too. He rubbed his face with his big hands, "It's…it's my baby, my daughter, she's…. she's pregnant Josh!" Joe said sadly. "Oh," Josh said, wondering why it was bad, "that's what's bothering you?" "Yeah, she's only seventeen, she's a baby herself! I tried to keep her from this, we home schooled her up until last year," he said, tapping a pencil on his desk. "She really wanted to get out into the "real world", and now look what happened!" he said, pressing his lips together. "Who is the father?" Josh asked and then regretted asking. "I don't want to talk about him!" Joe snarled. "What will she do now?" Josh asked, feeling totally unqualified for this conversation. "Well…. it's not the end of the world, but it will be hard for her. We'll help her with everything, of course, I just didn't think"…. Joe got choked up. Josh felt awkward but he stood up and walked over to Joe and put his hand on his shoulder. "I like babies, there really cute!" He had no idea where that came from. Joe started shaking. Josh thought he was crying, but he was actually laughing.

"Ah, you're right Josh… they are awfully cute aren't they?" he laughed. "I do love babies!" he said rubbing the tears from his eyes. "Guess that's why we had so many of them! I just didn't plan on being a "Papa bear" so soon, oh well! It's going to be alright!" Joe said, trying to comfort himself. "Like I said, it's not the end of the world, right Josh?" "That's right Joe!" Josh assured him. He was glad the mood had changed. "Hey Josh, how is your friend Kyle doing?" Joe asked. "He's doing a lot better, thanks for asking. Joe, I've been meaning to talk to you about something, if that's okay?" Josh asked. "Sure you can talk to me about anything, what's on your mind?" Joe said, as he leaned on the edge of his desk, looking right into Josh's eyes. "I've been having these dreams all week and um, they're so real and um, Jesus is in them," he said nervously. "Really, that's great!" Joe said. "Say, why don't you come to my house for dinner tonight, you can meet the family and we can discuss your dreams." he said, excited about the idea. "I'd love to Joe! What time should I be there?" Josh asked. "Let's say 6:00 sharp. Here's my address." Joe wrote down the address and handed it to Josh. "You're a good man Josh, thanks for listening to me about my little girl. I know you'll keep it to yourself," he said. "I won't tell anyone Joe, and thanks for the invitation, I'll be there on time!" he laughed. "Guess I better let my wife know!" Joe said picking up the phone and waving Josh out. "Hope it'll be okay with her!" he mumbled to himself.

"Mom, guess what…. my boss invited me over for dinner tonight!" Josh said as he hopped into the minivan. "Oh my, you know what that means don't you? A promotion, he's going to give you a promotion Josh!" she said excitedly. "He'll probably increase your pay by a dollar or two!" "Mom, you don't know that, and besides, what can I be promoted to, a cook?" he said. "A promotion is a promotion, don't knock it! You should wear the blue sweater I bought you last week and maybe the brown dress pants," she said. "Mom, I can dress myself, you don't need to tell me what to wear. I'm not a kid anymore!" he snapped. "Fine, fine, wear what you want! Just bring it down so I can iron it, okay "Mr. Grown Up!" They both laughed at that. "Where does he live?" she asked. Josh read the address to her. "That's the fancy neighborhood by the lake! I've drive past it on my way to work. They have privacy gates for security and it's full of big, beautiful homes with the prettiest landscaped lawns I've ever seen! I wish I could go with you! I'd love to see what their house looks like inside! You'll have to tell me all about it, look at everything closely so you remember, okay?" She went on and on, not waiting for an answer. Josh just rolled his eyes and smiled at her, he kind of liked the way she got excited over things in his life and he secretly liked all the attention she gave him. She made a big deal out of everything. But then, this was a big deal, he was actually going to meet "The Family" and he was starting to feel a little nervous about it.

They parked and went in the back door. Bethany came in the front door, threw her book bag on the floor and sulked as she plopped on the couch and opened her laptop. Josh was in a feisty mood and thought of a sure fire way to make her laugh. He ran to his bedroom, opened the closet door and rummaged around for his Halloween mask. Then he tiptoed into the kitchen and asked his mom for a large pot. "I'm going to put this in the pot and have Bethany open it!" he whispered to his mom. She loved to do this sort of thing so she was more than okay with his plan. She hid around the corner to watch Bethany's reaction, trying not to snicker too loud.

"Bethany, mom wants you to stir the soup!" Josh yelled from the stairs. "Why can't you do it?" she yelled back. "Just do it for her, I'm busy!" he yelled. She growled as she walked into the kitchen. She lifted the lid to the large pot and let out a scream as she fell backwards dropping the lid on the floor. Josh and Cami laughed hysterically when they saw what happened. "YOU MORON, you scared me to death!" she yelled. Josh grabbed the creepy head out of the pot and chased her with it. She jumped back on the couch and yelled, "Leave me alone!" "Aww, are you in a bad mood?!" he teased her some more. Then he ran around the corner, kicked off his shoes and slid on the wooden floor in front of her. He was using a pretend microphone singing loud and off key just to annoy her. "Leave me alone you weirdo!" she yelled. He jumped up and down on the couch, making her furious. "Am I a weirdo now? I'm going to drop a bomb on you!" he warned. She screamed, "get away from me!" She ran through the house with Josh chasing behind her, running and grunting like an ape.

He knocked her down in the kitchen and began dragging her through the house by her feet. "Mom, make him stop!" she said, half laughing and half crying. Cami was watching the mayhem and laughing herself then she saw her opportunity to act, when Josh stooped down to tickle his sister, she pushed him over and grabbed his foot, "Grab his other foot!" she told Bethany. Together they pulled Josh through the hallway. He easily escaped from them and chased Bethany through the house. She ran for cover behind the couch. He dove onto the couch. "CRACK" He had a look of horror on his face. "WHAT WAS THAT? Dog gone it Joshua, you broke the couch! I've told you a million times not to jump on it, now look what you've done!" his mother yelled. "Mom, mom, this is only a material object, I'm your son! This will soon fade away, but, but I'll be your son forever!" he said as he backed away from his angry mother. "If you kill me you won't get any treasure in Heaven!" he said as he ran for the stairs. "You better run before I catch you boy!"

she said. He started up the stairs and called back down, "And where did you get that terrible language young lady? Is "Dog gone it" in the Bible? What if Pastor Dan heard you talk like that?" Josh teased. She had to laugh at that even though she was still mad. She looked up and apologized to God then she walked to the stairway and called up to Josh. "I'm sorry I yelled at you Josh, you're more important to me than that old couch is," she said. "I'm sorry too, besides, that couch is ugly!" "You're such a bad boy! She laughed, *I wonder how he knew about having treasure in Heaven?"*

14

---∞∞∞---

The Car and the Garage

It was time for Josh to get ready for dinner at Joe's house. He looked through his closet for a nice shirt and ended up choosing the blue sweater that his mom had suggested but he didn't wear the brown pants because she wasn't going to run his life! Although he did have to borrow her minivan, which he thought was totally "lame".

He found the road that led to Joe's house, his mom was right, it was a nice place. The road had a lot of curves and hills and Josh enjoyed the drive. How he wished he was driving a sports car instead of the family van. The views were stunning as he caught glimpses of the lake through the large pine trees. *"God sure made the earth beautiful,"* he thought, *"I love the green grass and trees, the blue water and sky, it's all so perfect!"* Finally he saw Joe's house, a large log home on the hill in front of him. "Wow, now that's what I'm talking about!" he said out loud. The gate was made of huge logs and the driveway was long and curvy. The grounds, it wasn't a yard, it was much bigger than a yard, were absolutely beautiful. As he got closer he could see a boat dock down by the lake, a large horse stable, and an outdoor pool. He also spied a couple of four wheelers parked on the side of the house. *"He's living my dream!"* Josh thought. He wasn't sure if he should pull around back or park in the front, he decided on the front.

He walked up the long stone path to the massive wooden door. There were huge boulders on each side of the path with colorful flowers and bushes in between them. Joe even had a stream with a small waterfall flowing through his property. Josh found himself feeling green with envy. "*I didn't think Joe made this much money!*" he thought.

He stepped onto the front porch and rang the doorbell. The big door opened and there was what looked like the entire family gathered to greet him. "Why, hello Joshua, come in, come in!" said Joe's friendly wife. "Hey Josh, I'm glad you could come!" Joe said as he shook his hand. Then he introduced his family, "This is my wife Connie, my oldest son Wyatt, my middle son Jess, my oldest daughter, Cheyenne, and this is Dakota…." Josh nearly choked when he saw her. "You're the girl from the hospital!" he said. "Oh hi, you're Kyle's friend aren't you?" She was also surprised to see him. He couldn't believe it was her, he had been thinking about her ever since he saw her at the hospital. Joe interrupted and Josh made himself focus on what he was saying. Joe continued to introduce the younger kids, "This is Nevada, Marshall, Winslow and our baby John; we call him "The Duke." "It's nice to meet all of you. You have a nice family Joe, and a really beautiful home!" Josh said, sensing that Joe had a love for western things. "Why thank you Josh, it's very comfortable here," Joe said modestly. Josh thought to himself, "*I wonder which one is having a baby, Cheyenne or Nevada….or Dakota? Winslow is about ten, can't be her!*" "I'm making steaks on the grill, is that alright with you Josh?" Joe asked. "That sounds perfect Joe!" he answered. "Come out on the deck with me while I grill up these babies!" Joe said, grabbing the big platter of meat. "Josh honey, what would you like to drink? I have all the soft drinks, lemonade, or tea," Connie asked with a slightly southern accent. "Um, I'll take some lemonade please," he said politely.

Josh watched as Joe grilled the steaks. "I only flip em once, that's the secret to a juicy steak. How do you like your meat cooked Josh?" Joe asked. "Medium I guess," Josh replied. "Tell me about these dreams; I'm dying to hear about them!" Joe asked while tending to the steaks. They sat on the patio chairs and looked out over the rolling hills and the blue lake that was sparkling in the sun. "Well, in my dreams, which I've had every night since Friday, I find myself inside of my own heart, but it's also a house. And then Jesus shows up in every dream! He takes me on all these awesome adventures, and he talks to me about everything in my life. I'm learning all kinds of things from him, it's so cool and it all seems so real! What do you make of that Joe?" Josh asked. "Whoa, that is pretty cool! I've never heard of such a thing before. You're very blessed to have these dreams. God is revealing himself to you in a very special way. I wish I could have dreams like those!" he said. He seemed genuinely interested and not once did he tease Josh about it.

The time went fast and Josh had a great time with "The Family". They even played a game after dinner which seemed to be something they did regularly. All of Joe's kids were nice to him and they really seemed to like him, especially Dakota. After dinner, Joe invited Josh to have his dessert with him in his "man cave." It was a perfect room for a guy; the fireplace was huge and made of large smooth stones, over the mantle was a painting of cowboys on a cattle drive, and the furniture was large and made of the softest leather Josh had ever felt. The wood in the fireplace cracked and popped and it cast a soft glow on the walls. Joe got out his photo album that was full of pictures from Alaska. "If you ever get to go to Alaska, you should go salmon fishing, you'd love it! Here's Wyatt holding his first rifle. We went hunting up there two years ago. And that's Dakota and her mom standing on glacier ice in the middle of summer!" Joe wasn't trying to brag or show off at all, he just enjoyed life and wanted to share his experiences with others.

The two of them talked for quite some time while enjoying all the manly surroundings. "You really like western things don't you Joe? I'm surprised that you don't live in Montana or Wyoming." Josh said. "Maybe someday, but I like it here just fine. My wife's family all live around here and she would get too homesick if we moved away. You know what they say, "A happy wife makes a happy life!" Joe laughed. "That's sounds like good advice. I'll write that in my book, "Tips for poor single guys who don't have a clue, from rich, happily married men who have it all!" Josh said, trying to be funny. "Where'd you find that book?" Joe asked. "Oh, I was just kidding, there isn't any book like that." Josh answered. "Oh..., okay?" Joe looked at Josh with a confused expression. Josh wished he hadn't tried to be funny because Joe apparently didn't think he was. *"Dang it, there goes my promotion!"* he thought.

As they stared at the fire, Josh began to imagine what life would be like if he were to marry Dakota. *"I'd have a place like this and a family like Joe's. But, I think I'm in love with Kayla! Then again, Dakota is really good looking, but so is Kayla!"* His thoughts were tormenting him but he didn't show it. He asked a question that had been on his mind all night, "Joe, which daughter is having a baby? Hope you don't mind if I ask." "It's Dakota, my sweet little girl." That hit Josh like a ton of bricks. "Oh, um, I thought um…well I don't know what I thought." Josh was noticeably quiet after that. *"Now he really thinks I'm a dope!"* he thought.

"Well, Josh, I need to get up early." Joe said as he stood up, Josh stood up too. "Oh, wait, I have something to ask you. I need a cook in a bad way, would you like the job?" he asked. "Oh, that would be great Joe, but I don't know how to cook," Josh admitted. "Emanuel will teach you, he's one of the best! I'm moving him up to kitchen supervisor. Think about it, it's more hours and more money." Joe said. "I'll take it Joe, thank you!" Josh said without hesitation. "Great, I'll get you started next week! And if you're good at it I may let you transfer to my other restaurant." Joe said. "You have another restaurant?" Josh asked. "Yes, I own the Blue Harbor on the north side of the lake." Joe said, trying hard not to brag. "Wow, that's a nice place, or so I've been told." Josh said as he thought, *"No wonder Joe is rich, that place is expensive!"* "Well, I'll have to treat you and your family to dinner sometime. I think you'll like it." Joe said modestly. "My mom and sister would love that Joe!" Josh responded.

Joe and his family walked Josh to the door and said good night. He took one more look at Dakota before leaving. As he slowly drove home he thought about the evening at Joe's house. His mind was swirling and his emotions were driving him crazy. *"God, show me what to do, I'm so confused! I like Kayla a lot, a whole lot! But I like Dakota too! Then there's Kyle, he's going to get mad if he finds out that I am interested in Dakota. I don't know what to do!"* He thought again about what his life would be like if he was married to Dakota. He'd have the lifestyle he'd always dreamed of. *"Slow down, don't do anything yet. Right now you aren't seeing things clearly, so just wait for my guidance,"* said the voice of the Holy Spirit. *"Okay God, I'll wait, I don't know what else to do."*

When he got home, his mother was waiting for him. "So, how was it? Does he have a nice home?" she asked. "You wouldn't believe how nice it is mom! It's a big log home and it's really beautiful! And, you were right about the promotion, he wants me to be a cook! I start training next week and I'll get more hours and more money!" he said excitedly.

"That's great Josh, I'm so proud of you! Now you'll be able to buy us a new couch!" she laughed. They went on to talk about Joe's family. She wanted to know all their names, their ages, what they had for dinner and if it was good. She asked for every detail about the house and he tried hard to describe it all. "Oh yeah, Joe's going to take us all out to dinner at his other restaurant, The Blue Harbor," he said. "He owns The Blue Harbor? That's the best and the most expensive place around here! I've always wanted to go there!" She exclaimed. "I know, right! And he said he may transfer me there if I'm good enough, maybe I'll be the manager someday! Well, I have a busy day tomorrow I think I'll go to bed now," he said as he stood up and stretched. She hugged him and said, "You've had a lot going on this week, I bet you are tired!

He got cleaned up then sat on the edge of his bed and talked silently to God. *"I'm sorry I got jealous of all the cool things Joe has. I know you don't like that envy and jealousy stuff."* He was sleepy and in his thoughts began to ramble on and on.…. *"Why can't I stop thinking about Dakota? I know that Kyle likes her and I know she's going to have a baby, but ever since I saw her in the hospital she's been on my mind! And now I find out that she's Joe's daughter! But I'm way too young to get married and have a family, what am I thinking?! Besides, when I do settle down, Kayla is the one I want to be with, I think!"* He let out a loud groan as he laid back and covered his head with his pillow and punched it in frustration. He'd never felt like this before. How could he have strong feelings, maybe love, for two girls at the same time? He beat up on his pillow again, growling and biting it like a grizzly bear. His mom heard it as she walked past his room. She knocked lightly on his door and asked, "You alright Josh?" "Oh, yeah I'm…. trying to…get comfortable. Good night mom," he said sheepishly. Soon after, he fell into a deep sleep.

"Josh, can you come into the garage please?" Jesus peeked around to the backyard where Josh was standing. Josh smiled and said, "Sure, I'll be right there!" He was happy to be back in his dream world. As he came around the corner he saw a beautiful red sports car convertible. "Is this my car?" he asked excitedly. "It's all yours my boy!" Jesus said as he put an arm around him.. "Oh, and I have one more surprise for you, meet Gabe, your guardian," he said pointing to the large angel. Josh turned around to see an enormous angel standing behind him. "Hi Gabe, it's nice to meet you," he said as he held out his shaky hand, "Haven't we met before?" he asked. "Aww, come here, I've waited a long time to do this!" Gabe said as he hugged Josh up off the ground. "Be careful Gabe, you'll crush him!" Jesus laughed. "You sure have kept me busy Josh between saving you from car wrecks and falling rocks, I barely have time to catch my breath!" Gabe said. "Really, you've saved my life?" Josh was amazed to hear that. "Yes, Gabe has come between you and death quite a few times!" Jesus responded. "It wasn't your time yet." Gabe added with a big smile. Josh and Gabe both jumped when Jesus revved the engine of the car. "Want to go for a spin?" he asked. "Sure, where are we going?" Josh asked. "God only knows!" Gabe replied as he hopped in the back. "Hey, can I drive?" Josh asked. Jesus got out and walked around the car and opened Josh's door. "Okay you can drive." Jesus got in and tuned the radio to KLOVE, his favorite station. A song came on, *"OUR GOD'S NOT DEAD, HE'S SURELY ALIVE"* "I love the News Boys!" he said as he put on his sunglasses and sang along.

They drove through town honking and waving at the people walking by. "Let's see what she can do, turn this way," Jesus pointed to a road that led them out into the country. He turned to Josh and said, "This is a dream, you can speed in dreams. Go ahead, punch it!" Josh put it in gear and stepped on the gas, they flew down the road, laughing and singing. The road curved around like a snake but Josh handled it like a professional racer. He slowed down a bit and looked over at Jesus to get his reaction. Jesus turned toward him, smiled and said, "You've got good reflexes and control, let me show you how to control yourself as well as you do this car." Josh just smiled, not sure what to say to that.

They rode along in silence for a while, finally Josh had to ask, "What do you mean by that, why do you need to teach me to control myself?" Jesus smiled, pulled down his sunglasses and said, "You can be very impulsive. I'd like you to get my advice about everything. I can help you make the right decisions. Take David, you know David, from the Bible?" he asked. Josh shook his head. "David and Goliath, you know?" Jesus asked. "Oh, yeah, I know who you're talking about." Josh said. "He became King over Israel and he humbled himself before me, knowing that he was made of flesh and blood, he knew he needed my help and guidance. When the enemies threatened to attack, he would always ask me what to do. That's what I want you to do. I am your councilor after all. I know what's best for you and I can show you what road to take, metaphorically and literally. Josh just smiled and shook his head in agreement.

They then discussed where to stop for lunch. Josh suggested a place down by the lake. "That's perfect! I have someone there that I want you to meet," Jesus replied. They enjoyed the wind blowing through their hair as they drove along the winding road. The road was smooth and Josh loved driving his new car on it. It handled like a dream, but the dream was about to turn into a nightmare......

The strangest thing happened, the nice smooth blacktop road turned into sand! It was banked like a racetrack, high on one side. Josh couldn't get his car to move through the thick sand and his tires were spinning and spraying it everywhere! "What happened to the road Jesus?" he asked. He turned to look but Jesus was gone. Then he turned to ask Gabe but he wasn't there either. "Where are you guys?" he yelled as he got out of the car and began to walk, it was hard because the sand was so deep. Looking up, he saw a farm house in the distance and two women working in a flower bed. "Hello, can you help me?" he called to them. As he approached them he noticed that they were both bending over picking flowers and putting them into baskets. They both had on long dresses and sunhats. "Can you tell me where I am?" he asked as he walked into the garden. The young women both stood up straight and turned to look at him.

To his surprise it was Kayla and Dakota! "What are you doing here Josh?" they asked. "My car is stuck in that sand dune over there," he said pointing to the car. "Can one of you give me a ride home?" he asked. "I'll take you home Josh," Kayla said. "No, I'll take him!" Dakota protested. The two of them began to fight over who would drive him home. Then he heard some yelling behind him. He looked around and saw a gang of farmers dressed in overalls bursting out of a big red barn. They all started running toward him, each of them holding a shovel or a pitch fork. They looked like ghoulish versions of Kyle and Joe and all of his sons. They were yelling at Josh and they looked really mad about something. He turned to run away but his feet were so slow that he could barely move them, so he got down on the ground and began crawling on his stomach like a soldier making his way through a mine field.

When he finally reached the car he realized that it wasn't a car anymore, it was an old broken down airplane. The farmers were fast approaching as he climbed into the cockpit. He tried to start the engine. The propellers were turning a little and the engine was sputtering. "Come on, start you piece of junk!" he yelled. Suddenly it started and the propellers began to spin faster and faster, the engine roaring louder and louder. Before he knew it the plane was rolling down a runway! The mob of angry farmers was chasing after him, throwing pitch forks at the plane. With a strong pull on the throttle, the plane lifted off the ground and soared into the bright blue sky. But he was terrified to see that some of the farmer zombies had hung on to the wings and were inching their way toward him. Some were crawling into plane! They seemed to be everywhere! It was like some bad video game. "Get off, get off of me!" he yelled as he tried to peal one of the farmers off of his back. "I can't breathe, get off of me you big gorilla!"

He finally managed to shove the man off, but all that wrestling around made him lose control and the plane went into a nosedive. "HELP, HELP ME GABE!!!! He yelled. "I can't pull out of this, GOD WHERE ARE YOU?" he cried as he pulled back on the throttle as hard as he could. The control panel was flashing and alarms were going off. He peeked and saw the ground getting closer and closer, he could even see his own house as he sped toward it. "THIS IS IT! I'M A DEAD MAN!" he cried as he closed his eyes tightly and braced for the impact. "CRASH!" He fell out of his bed, knocking over the night stand and lamp, getting tangled up in the sheets and blankets. The table and lamp ended up on top of him too. "What… what happened to my plane? Am I dead?" He gasped for air and sat up. After sitting in the dark a few seconds his mind slowly cleared and he saw the familiar surroundings of his room. "Oh, it was just a dream, thank God!"

He took a deep breath and exhaled slowly trying to calm himself. "These dreams are getting pretty intense Jesus!" he said, wiping tears of fear from his eyes. "And where did you go, why did you bale on me?" he asked in a loud angry whisper. *"Even when you can't see me or hear me or feel my presence, I'm with you! Learn to trust in me more,"* he heard the Spirit say to him. "That dream really scared me! Does it mean I'm not supposed to date Kayla or be interested in Dakota?" he asked. *"Take one step at a time Josh, follow me and I'll teach you how to control your thoughts and feelings. You can't trust them anyway, they change all the time! But I never change and my word never changes, you can rely on it!"* Jesus said. "Okay, okay I'll try to follow you, but my mind doesn't work that way. I've always been impulsive and I've made a lot of mistakes, I know, but I like calling the shots. It's hard to know what to do with my life, which road to take, you know what I mean?" *"I know Josh, just be patient, I'll show you the way to go if you'll let me."* Jesus said. "Just one question, how will I know which girl is for me?" Josh asked. The Spirit of God answered with a vision. Josh clearly saw Kayla's face. "Awesome, thanks Jesus, and next time, you can drive!" he said as he rubbed the bump on his head.

Josh set the table and lamp back in place and threw the sheets and blankets back on his bed. He glanced at the clock. It was 2:11 in the morning. Still feeling a little shaken by his dream, he decided to go down to the kitchen for a glass of orange juice or something. *"What a crazy dream!"* He thought about it as he sat on the stool dipping a cookie in a tall glass of milk. His mind started wandering again and he began envisioning what his life might be like being married to Kayla, and then his thoughts shifted back to Dakota. He thought about what their kids might look like. But before he got too carried away with his daydreams, he snapped out of it. *"Oh brother, this is getting ridiculous!"* he thought. *"Okay Jesus, show me how to control my thoughts, I need help! Hello, can you hear me?"* *"I hear you Joshua. Take out your sword and use it! Remember you can take your thoughts captive.... and make them obey me!"*

Josh went back to his room and took his bible. He opened it, trying to find a verse to meditate on. He found two good ones:

Psalm 119:105 "Your word is a lamp to my feet and a light for my path."

John 16:13 "But when he, the Spirit of truth comes, he will guide you into all truth....

He read the verses over and over until he memorized them. Then he got out of bed and sat down at his desk. He took out a pad of paper and a pen and began to write down all of his dreams. *"I hope these dreams never stop. I enjoy them, even the scary ones!"* he thought as he tried to get all of the details in order. Then he remembered the dream he had about building the chest for Karly and her baby, so he made a note to himself to actually do it. He also remembered Jesus had said that there was someone he wanted him to meet down by the lake. He wrote it down and put a star by it. After about a half hour he started getting sleepy. He put his things away and slipped back under his blankets then peacefully drifted off to a place he had come to love, his heart land.

15

———— ⚬⚬⚬ ————

The Front Yard

It was bright and sunny outside. Josh went to the kitchen sink for a glass of water, he pulled the curtains to the side and saw the neighbor kids playing in the yard, they liked to congregate in his yard because he was so much fun and they all loved him. He always had a fun game to play or a good story to tell, plus, he had the coolest play fort in the neighborhood. He slipped on his shoes and ran outside to greet them, "Hi kids!" he yelled. "Joshua, Joshua!" the kids screamed with delight as they all ran to him, encircling him with hugs. He got down on his hands and knees and yelled, "Climb on everybody!" They all tried, but only two of them could fit on his back. "Hee-haw, hee-haw" he called out as he bucked around the yard like a donkey. Then he got up and chased them around the front yard. After several games of tag and hide-n-seek, they took a little break under the shady maple tree.

"Hey kids" he said as they all collapsed on the ground, everyone out of breath. "What Josh?" they all asked. "Someone very special has moved into my house," he said. "Who is it Josh?" they squealed with excitement. "It's Jesus, God's son!" he replied. That started a flurry of questions, "God has a son? What does he look like? Is he nice? Can we meet him?" "Wait, wait, I think I'm going to have a party soon and I'll invite all of you and your parents over to meet him, would you like that?" he asked. "Yes, that would be awesome!" they shouted in unison. "Can we play games and have cake and ice cream?" one of them asked. "Sure, we can do that," he said with a laugh. "I'm sure Jesus likes cake and ice cream. Maybe you can talk him into playing games with us, I hear he's pretty good at…..well, he's actually good at all of them!" Josh laughed.

"Now, everyone gather around me, I'm going to tell you a couple of stories about him," Josh said as he quieted them down. He proceeded to tell them stories he had just read in his Bible and a few he had personally experienced in the last few days. "I know for a fact that Jesus loves babies and children, you are very special to him. Why, just the other day he told me that Heaven, the place where he lives, is full of children! He's made playgrounds for you and I'll bet they're way, way better than any we have here on Earth! And because he loves you so much, he wants you to love him too, he's a good God and he wants you to know that. Jesus became one of us. He was born a human baby. And he grew to be a child, just like you, he experienced the same things you do; hurt feelings, runny noses…" "Did he get owies too?" asked a three year old. "I'm sure he got owies and he had a mommy who kissed them, just like your mommy does!" he answered. "I can't wait for you to meet him, you're going to love him!" he said. Then he stood up and gave them each a big hug, and spun them around before he sent them home. "Bye Joshua, see you tomorrow, love you!" they called out. "Love you too!" he called back.

"Knock-knock" "Josh, do you want some breakfast before your ball practice?" his mother asked. He opened his eyes and realized he'd had another dream. "Ah, yeah, that'd be good, thanks mom," he said. It took a few minutes before he even felt like moving. He walked over to the dresser and pulled out a clean pair of socks and his baseball uniform then headed for the bathroom when he heard loud voices coming from the back yard. He went to the window to look. There were kids in the yard! *That's weird, what are they doing out here? It's just like the dream,* he thought. Then he quickly got dressed and ran down stairs to find out who they were. His mom was in the kitchen talking to a young woman. "Josh, this is Melissa, she and her family just moved to the neighborhood," she said. "Hi Melissa it's nice to meet you," he said, holding out his hand to shake hers. "Hi Josh, I'm glad to meet you too. My boys were dying to play in your yard! You sure have a nice play area!" She said. "Oh yeah, my dad built that for us years ago, we're all too old for it now," he said. "Well, it will be nice for your children, I mean, when you have children," she added. "Oh, that won't be for a long, long time!" he laughed. "Would you like to meet my boys?" she asked. "Sure, I'd love to meet them."

They walked out to the yard where the boys were playing. "Ryan and Brady, this is our new neighbor Josh, and you already met his mother," Melissa said. "Hi Josh, you have a cool yard!" They said. "Thanks boys, come with me and I'll show you my secret passages and my spaceship/ pirate ship/fighter jet!" Josh said proudly. "Oh boy, let's go!" Ryan yelled excitedly. "I love to see them play and use their imagination," Melissa said. "Well, they'll have fun playing with Josh then, he's got a great imagination and sometimes I wonder if he's ever going to grow up!" Cami laughed. The two of them returned to the kitchen and to their coffee. Meanwhile out in the play fort, Josh was explaining to the boys what all of the homemade gadgets were. "This stick is your throttle, and this is the control panel and this is how you steer the jet."

Brady got a serious look on his face and said, "Uh Josh, I think this is a "Transformer." "Brady, it's his fort!" Ryan corrected his younger brother. "No, I think he's right Ryan, it is a "Transformer!" Josh winked at Ryan. Ryan was five years older than Brady. And even though Brady was only five, the two of them played good together, most of the time.

Josh hadn't been up in the tree house for years. He looked at all the things he had added to the fort when he was a kid and it surprised him how well he had made them. "You guys are welcome to play here anytime. You just have to ask your mom first, and mine, okay?" he said. "Okay, thanks Josh!" Ryan and Brady were thrilled to have a cool place like this to play in.

"Boys, we need to go now." Melissa called up to them. "I have to go too, but I'll see you soon." Josh promised the boys. He climbed down the ladder following the boys. "Thanks for showing them around Josh, I'm sure they had fun," she said. Josh and his mom really liked Melissa and the boys. They had yet to meet her husband Kevin. He had a great career and he made enough money to allow Melissa to be a stay at home mom. She did a great job raising the boys and she knew how important it was to be at home with them. Now that they were both in school all day, she decided to go to work part time as a counselor for troubled teens. She mentioned it to Josh and Cami. "That's wonderful, where is your clinic located?" Cami asked.

"I'm going to have an office in one of the beautiful old Victorian houses on Main Street, across from the Vintage Café." Melissa replied. "Oh, it must be one of the Six Sisters. The Seven Brothers are on the other side of the street," Cami said. "What, I grew up here and I never heard about the "sisters and brothers", what are you talking about?" he asked. "Oh, I'm sorry honey… I thought I told you about them. They were the sons and daughters of the man and his wife who helped settle this town. They each made their mark on Angel Cross, making a lot of money for themselves and for the town back in their day. They all loved it here so much that they each had a home built on Main Street. All of those beautiful Queen Ann Victorian homes were built by them," she explained. "They must have gotten along really well to want to live side by side like that," Melissa laughed. "Ah, for a while they did. Two of the brothers went away to war and never returned. I've heard lots of great stories about them, good and bad," Cami said. She asked Melissa if she had ever heard the story of how the town got its name, Angel Cross. She hadn't heard about it but she was fascinated by all of the stories and she wanted to hear more but she had to leave. "I'm so glad to have nice neighbors like you!" she said as she gathered the boys and headed home. "I like her, she's going to be a good friend, I can tell." Cami said with a smile.

Josh became very interested to hear about the family that helped settle his home town. He had always thought about world history but never about local history, now he just had to look into it for himself. "So mom, what's their name, the parents of all those sisters and brothers?" he asked "It was Henry and Margaret Cook. They built one of the first log cabins in the settlement. Henry also helped build the old stone mill down by the river and he and Margaret started up the very first store in town," she said. "Where have I heard those names, I know I've heard those names!" Josh asked himself. "Maybe from your teacher?" his mother asked. "No, that's not it." He thought while scratching his head. "Oh, I know where I've seen the names… I mow around their graves! How cool is that!" he laughed. "That is pretty cool Josh! I have a book about them if you want to read it sometime," she offered. "Great, then I can find out all about old Henry and his wife Margaret, thanks mom!" Then he asked, "How *did* the town get the name "Angel Cross"?" "Oh, Joshua, I've told you about that a hundred times, so did your grandma and grandpa!" she said. "You mean the story about the old woodcarver? I thought you all just made that up!" he said. "No, it's all true! Just go downtown and read the plaque on the corner of Main and 1st Street." she said. She couldn't say much about Josh because she never paid much attention to that stuff either when she was his age.

The old story Josh heard went like this: It was many years ago, in the month of November, 1835, one year and three months after the town was first settled, that a huge blizzard blew in. The storm was so big that the snow completely covered the houses and it came half way up the barns. Everyone was trapped, buried in a thick blanket of new snow. The blizzard caught them off guard, it came before snow usually fell in these parts and it took everyone by surprise. It was a blinding snowstorm and they couldn't see two feet in front of themselves. On that particular day, seventeen people were out and about. Some went to the neighboring town to buy supplies, some were out in the woods chopping firewood, and some of the children were fishing or playing down by the lake. One woman was taking a pie to the new pastor and his family who lived on the edge of the woods. It took hours for the townsfolk just to dig themselves out of their own homes. They searched everywhere for their missing children and friends. Then the pastor of the town called everyone together to pray for help in finding the missing loved ones.

Two days had gone by with no sign of any of them. Then on the third day they started showing up. One by one or two at a time they made their way through the deep snow back to the tiny town of Harris. The amazing thing was that each of them told how they had been rescued by an old wood carver who lived in a cabin in the middle of the woods. He had fed and sheltered them, but not all them together. They said that they had been in his cabin alone or with one other person who was with them, but never more than two of them. The old man showed them the way to get home but didn't come with them past the woods. Another amazing thing about the story was that each of them was wearing a wooden cross necklace, hand carved by the old man himself. And each of the crosses had a different word carved into it. The pastor of the town examined the crosses and realized that each word was a name or title for Jesus.

After the snow melted the whole town set out to find the old man and thank him, but no one ever found him. There was no cabin, and no trace of anyone living in the woods. They all knew it was a miracle and that God had sent an angel to save those that were lost in the blizzard. The whole town met in the little church and voted to rename their town "Angel Cross" so that they would always remember the miracle that happened in the winter storm of 1835. Now some of the crosses have been placed in a small museum in the middle of town and others have been handed down from one generation to the next. There were 17 crosses in all, one given to each of the people who were caught in the storm.

Josh thought about that story again. Then he suddenly remembered something. "MOM, I have one of those crosses! Not one of the original 17, but I have one! Remember when we were camping and I got lost in the woods trying to get help for Kyle? There was that old guy, I think he was fishing by the river, he saw me crying because I was lost. He gave me a wooden cross, and I still have it!" he didn't wait for her to respond, he raced up to his room and tore his closet apart searching for his old cigar box full of his boyhood treasures, he found it under a stack of old books.

Sitting on the edge of his bed, he slowly opened the box, praying that the old necklace was still in there. He gasped when he saw the leather cord. Carefully, he removed the other things that were lying on top of it, "There it is!" he said excitedly. His mom walked in the room. "You really have a wooden cross?" she sounded shocked. "I never told you because he told me to keep it a secret," Josh held up the old cross and read it, "Look, it says, "Good Shepherd", is that one of Jesus' names?" he asked. "Yeah, it is. I'll show you!" She took his Bible and turned to the story Jesus told about the good shepherd. It was a description of how God searches for his lost sheep, or people. "This is so cool! I can't believe that old guy was an angel, that's amazing!" he laughed. His mother was equally amazed by it. They carefully wrapped the necklace in tissue paper and placed it in a special wooden box for safe keeping.

Josh then headed off to ball practice on his bike. He deliberately rode down Main Street so he could take a closer look at all the old Victorian houses. They were all in excellent condition. Each one was beautifully painted which showed the detail of the woodwork, and each of the houses had a big maple tree in the front, which Josh assumed were all planted at the same time because they all were the same size and they were perfectly spaced. The yards had either a white picket fence or a black wrought iron fence and each yard had colorful flowers and bushes that were neatly trimmed. He felt proud that these houses were in his home town, they helped make it even more charming and attractive. Most of the old houses were private residences, but a few had become businesses. There was the Vintage Cafe, the travel agency, the clinic, a bed and breakfast, and an antique shop. Josh glanced past the houses and saw the historical marker on the corner of the street, under the old fashioned street lamp. It was a large bronze plaque. He had noticed it before, but he never actually read it. Walking his bike, he approached it, and read,

"This marks the sight of "The Big Prayer Meeting" On November 28, 1835 all the residents of Harris gathered together to pray for the men, women and children who were caught in the blizzard. On November 25, 1835, a large snow storm buried the town. Seventeen people were missing.

It went on to tell about the wood carver and how he guided the missing people to safety. Then it told how the people voted to change the name of the town to Angel Cross. And at the end was this prayer:

We thank God and praise him for the abundant blessings he has given and for the protection he provides for us all. He has heard and answered our prayers and he has sent his angel to help us. We pray that each new generation of Angel Cross will know the comfort and peace that the Lord has bestowed on us this day. And may we always remember and give thanks for the miracle of the Guardian Angel, the one that God has given the task of watching over us now and forever. In the name of Jesus our Lord we ask it. Amen.

"Wow, that's an amazing story!" he thought. Suddenly he felt warm all over as an inner peace, love and joy began filling him up from his feet to the top of his head. He smiled as it welled up and overflowed, he knew it must be from God. "Thank you sending them the angel and thank you for my angel," he said quietly. He began to feel a connection to the people who had lived here so many years ago and a strong sense of belonging. As he rode to the baseball park, he smiled to see the name of his team, "The Guardians"; it meant much more to him now. He grabbed his glove and walked toward the ball diamond, stopping short when he noticed his team mate Mike's last name printed on his shirt, "Cook". He had seen it many times before, but now he wondered if Mike might be related to Henry and Margaret Cook.

"Hey Josh, it's your turn at bat!" someone yelled. He had been daydreaming and it took a second for him to clear his mind. The peace, love and joy he felt earlier began to evaporate into the hot sun and he let out a loud sigh, wishing he could keep that feeling all of the time. "Nice hit Josh!" the coach yelled as Josh slugged the ball over the fence. "Why don't you hit like that when we're actually in a game?" some of the guys teased. "I hit better than all of you losers!" he teased back.

He sat on the bench next to Mike and asked him about his last name, "Hey Mike, are you related to the Cooks that founded Angel Cross?" "Ah, I think so, my mom talks about that stuff sometimes but I never really pay attention to her, you know?" he answered. "Yeah, I do that too, sometimes when my mom goes on and on about boring stuff I tune her out. But now she's got me interested in the history of the town. She has a book about it. I'll let you know if I read anything about your family in it," Josh said as he twirled a bat on his finger. "My mom said something about some runaway slaves that my distant relatives hid in their barns," Mike recalled. "That's cool, maybe I can talk to your mom sometime. I'd like to hear about that." Josh said. "Oh, she'd love that, but be prepared to have her talk your ear off!" Mike laughed. Music played in his pocket, it was his cell phone. "Hey Dakota, what's up? No, I can't right now, I'm at ball practice. Well, you're going to have to figure that out. It's not my problem! Yeah, well you can tell your dad that I'm busy! Now leave me alone!" he said in a hateful tone.

Josh's eyes widened as he overheard Mike talking. *"I wonder if it's the same Dakota I know? He's being a real jerk to her!"* he thought as his face grew red with anger. Mike hung up the phone and swore loudly. "Is everything alright?" Josh asked. He didn't really know Mike that well, but he was dying to find out if he was talking to the same Dakota that he knew. "This girl is driving me crazy! I wish she'd just leave me alone! She's going to have a kid, but I don't want to be a dad yet, you know?" he said. Josh turned his head and tried to control his temper. He only responded with a grunt, but he was thinking, *"you should have thought about that before, you moron! What should I say to him God?"* he wondered. Then the words came from somewhere within him, "I think I may know this girl," he said. Then he asked what her last name was. "Yep, I met her the other night, I work for her father. She seems like a really nice girl and she has a great family." He paused to think, "Maybe you're not ready to be a father, but Dakota's going to be a mother to the baby…., with or without you. I don't know what to tell you man, but I think you should at least help her and try to be nice to her. You didn't sound very nice on the phone, man. I'm sure you're confused, but so is she! She's got a little baby to take care of, man! It's got to be scary for her. Just take it easy on her, okay?" he said softening his voice. Mike hung his head and didn't say anything for a while. Then he spoke quietly to Josh, "You're right Josh, I've been a real jerk to her. I guess I am confused and maybe a little scared too," he said.

The two of them got quiet and watched the game for a while. Then Mike spoke again, "I just don't know what to do about all of this. I'm not ready to get married or take care of a baby! I don't even have a job! And my parents would kill me if they knew!" he said as he stood up. "Hey, thanks for talking to me about this. I've kept it all inside. It's good to talk to someone about it. Can you tell coach that I'm not feeling well? I think I need to take a walk and think," he said "Sure, I'll tell him," Josh stood up and put his arm around Mike's shoulder and said, "Hey man, if you need to talk, you can call me, I'll be there for you." Then he sent his number to Mike's phone. Just think about what I said, okay?" he said. "I will, thanks man," Mike said as he slowly walked away. As Josh watched him go, he started to feel a strange compassion for Mike, he thought, *"This feeling must be coming from you God because I would have kicked his butt!"* "You're up Josh!" he heard someone yell, "Try to hit the ball this time!" "What are talking about," he said, "didn't you see me hit that last one? You're just jealous, that's all!" he laughed. He started to walk to the mound then stopped short, the love, joy and peace hadn't left him, they were stirring around, deep within him. He smiled and thought, *"You really are in my heart! I can feel you tinkering around down there. Hey Jesus, if I have any, could you send up some of that patience that you talked about earlier, I could sure use some right now."*

16

The Fruit Tree

After practice Josh headed home. He was really hungry so he stopped for lunch at the "Root beer Barrel", a local fast food joint. He sat alone in a booth eating two chilidogs, an order of onion rings and a large root beer. Between bites he texted Kayla. He asked her if she would like to watch his game later that night. She said she would and she asked if two her friends, Madison and Grace could come along. He said yes, and said that he would take them out for ice cream after the game. "Great, see you later tater!" she texted. "LOL, you're my sweet patater!" he responded. "Meet me there at 7:00, we're playing at the "River Hawk stadium tonight."

After spending the afternoon online looking for car parts, he took a shower and put on his clean uniform. "You coming to the game mom?" he asked as he held up her keys. "No, I'm sorry honey. I'm going with my friends, Bonnie, Vicky and Betsy to see a tribute band down at the band shell in the park. You take the van and go, they're picking me up." she said. He felt a little let down because he secretly liked having an audience of adoring fans. "Okay, I'm meeting Kayla and her friends for ice cream after, I won't be too late," he said as he headed out the back door. "I won't be late either!" she called out, "I have a life too!" she laughed to herself.

The night was perfect for a ball game, not too hot, with a slight breeze to blow the sweat away. The sun was slowly setting after the third inning and the lights came on. Josh loved night games, the sound of the music, the excitement of the fans, and the glow of the field, the smells

127

of popcorn and hotdogs that filled the air. It was surreal, almost ghostly down there on the diamond. They were playing the Richmond Rockets, which was a very tough team to beat. The score was Richmond 2, Angel Cross 1. Josh had hit a couple of nice ones out to center field only to have them caught by a guy who ran like a cheetah. It was the Guardians turn at bat, the bases were loaded and Mike was up. "Come on Mike, over the fence!" Josh yelled. Mike hit two foul balls. "Wait for it Mike!" the coach yelled. "SMACK" went the ball as it hit the catcher's mitt. Mike struck out. "Your bat Josh, hit it over!" the coach yelled. Josh readied himself with his routine; he tapped his shoes with the bat, he crouched down, held the bat way back, rolled it around a couple of times, his eyes were on the ball, SWING!" "Take your time, make him pitch to you Josh!" yelled Jared as he warmed up. Then Josh connected with a perfect pitch and hit the ball right past the pitcher. As he dove for first base, his helmet flew off and he slammed into the first basemen's side. He saw it coming right for his head but he couldn't move fast enough. The ball hit him right above his left eye.

He woke up in a large bed, an old bed with heavy velvet covers and dark wooden posts on all four corners. The same type of heavy material made a canopy around the whole bed. "Where am I?" he said out loud. He jumped when a black hooded figure peeked in at him. "Have I died, are you the death angel?" he squeaked. Jesus laughed and pulled off the hood. "Oh, Lord, you scared me for a second!" he exhaled in relief. "I've come to show you some things about the spiritual fruit, love. I thought we'd do it like the story of "Scrooge", sort of. Instead of the spirits of the past, present and future, you'll have me, the Holy Spirit. I'll show you "love" in action, love is a verb, remember that. We'll see the whole spectrum of love. But first I'll take you to see hatred in its many forms, none of them are pleasant to watch, but you need to see the contrast between hate and love first hand, there's nothing like on the job training.

Take my hand," he said, reaching out to Josh. Suddenly they were flying over the night sky of old London, why London, why not? They soared over the ocean in a flash and landed smoothly on the street corner of a small town in the southern part of America.

"Okay Josh, observe hatred on a small scale," the Spirit said as he pointed to the people coming toward them. "They can't see us," he said.

"Listen to their conversation." A young white couple walked down the sidewalk dressed in casual clothes that looked to be from the 1920's or 1930's. An older black man was approaching from the opposite direction. "What you doing walking on this sidewalk? When we walk by, you step off! You got no business on this sidewalk. Get off now!" the white man yelled in a hateful tone, his wife shaking her head in agreement, "You heard him, go on now, shoo!" she said as if he were a pesky fly.

They were talking down to the man who was just passing by. Instead of showing any respect for the man's age, they treated him like an animal. The older gentleman quietly stepped down to the street and let them pass. It was hard for Josh to watch this happen. "What a… jerk!" he said, as he clenched his teeth and his fists. He walked over to the young white man, "Who do you think you are?" he yelled in his ear. "He can't hear you Josh, come with me," the Spirit said whisking him away. They flew back over the ocean and landed in a dirty room filled with hooded men who held automatic weapons and had bombs strapped to their chests. They were talking loudly to a classroom full of small children. "It is your duty and honor to kill as many dirty Jews as you can! If you die killing them, "god" will reward you in paradise!" they promised. The children were being taught to hate and to kill, for their "god". Josh shook his head and said, "What kind of "god" do they serve, it sure isn't you Jesus, you're a God of love! This is unbelievable, why do they have so much hatred for the Jews?" he asked. The Spirit didn't answer. He just grabbed Josh's hand and said, "It's time to show you hatred on a large scale."

They flew over what looked to be a large bubbling cauldron. Josh gasped and held his nose as the putrid odor rose and stung his nostrils. He coughed as he spoke, "What is this horrible place?" he asked. The Spirit pointed in the direction of swarm of ghastly creatures. As they approached, Josh could hear their hideous voices. "What are they doing?" he asked. "They are planning how best to destroy mankind, that includes you Josh. They are the fallen ones, Satan and his followers. "What a bunch of losers!" Josh said as he scanned the crowd. "They're losers alright. They lost everything when they rebelled against me, they thought they could defeat me, imagine that! They hate mankind because you are my special creation and because I love you, but they hate me more than they hate you." The Spirit used a sweeping motion with his arm and said, "This is the source of hatred as well as great evil and wickedness. People throughout history have heard these followers of Satan whisper wicked and cruel ideas into their minds. Many have done the things that they have heard and have put those wicked thoughts into action. Enough of this! Come see what love can do!" the Spirit said, taking Josh's arm.

They flew back to the area where they had witnessed the scene between the older man and the young couple. This time, Josh saw a young white woman. She was running through the woods alone and crying. Somehow he knew that she was running away from home and from the father who had beaten and abused her ever since she was a small girl. Josh watched as she jumped over logs and scratched her legs on some thorny bushes. Barefoot and thirsty, she came upon a group of old, run down cabins. She slowed to a stop when she realized that she had run right into the *"colored"* people's homestead. It frightened her when several people came out to see what the dogs were barking about. Wanting to run, but too afraid to move, she figured these people must hate her because of all the mean things that white folks did and said to them. She was shaking as an older man approached her with his hand extended.

"You hurt ma'am? Let me *hep* you. Come sit on my porch and rest *fo* a while," he said in a soft voice. "I get you some water. Is you hungry Miss?" he asked, being very kind and gentle to her. Everyone gathered around to see her and they seemed so eager to help her. It was like they wanted to prove to her that they were good people. They fed her, washed off the cuts and gave her some cold well water to drink. Then the old man took her by the hand and with tears in his eyes, he prayed for her to be safe. "You better git now young lady. Be bad if they *catches* you here with us. God be with you," he said. "Thank you sir, and thank you everyone!" she said.

She waved good-bye as she slipped into the woods and disappeared. Josh looked at Jesus, the Holy Spirit and said, "That was the same old man we saw earlier! He was so nice to that girl. I don't understand why he would do that, the white people hate him!" "No, not all of them hate him. Wasn't that beautiful, I love that!" Jesus said. "Come, see more love

Josh!" They flew back to the Middle East and landed in a clean hospital room in Tel-Aviv, Israel. In the room, doctors and nurses worked to help a little boy who had a severe pain in his stomach. The boy had attended the school where Josh had heard the terrorists spewing out their hatred into the children's minds. The boy's father and mother turned to the people of Israel for help. They had heard how skilled the staff was at this hospital and how good they had treated others in need.

As Josh looked on, he saw the mother embrace the doctor and nurse who had helped her little boy. "Love wins over hate every time! Love your enemies Josh," the Spirit smiled broadly. They watched as the little boy slept in the peaceful hospital room which was run by those he had been taught to hate. The Spirit walked over and kissed the boy's cheek and brushed the hair from his face then he walked over to his sleeping parents and touched them on the head, "Dream of me, I love you." he whispered into their ears. "One more Josh, come with me," he said. They flew through space where the stars were shining brighter than Josh had ever seen them shine before. The Spirit stopped and turned to look at him then he pulled back a large airy curtain that looked like the Northern Lights. "Just a peek!" he said as he revealed a whole new realm to Josh's eyes. Josh gasped at the beauty of what he saw and heard behind the curtain that looked like it was made of the fabric of space itself. All of his senses were bombarded with what he was experiencing. Then he saw him! He was magnificent to behold! It was Jesus, smiling and laughing and shining as bright as the stars. Then Jesus spoke. It was a voice that sounded like a mighty waterfall and yet it was very warm and friendly. "I can hardly wait Abba Father, I am ready to go to my beloved bride and bring her here where she will live with me forever!" he said as he strode majestically into the throne room that was so beautiful it was beyond imagination. "Soon my son, the preparations are nearly finished. It will be a magnificent wedding my dear son!" Josh heard the booming yet happy voice say. He knew it was the voice of the Father himself.

"That's all I can show you," the Spirit said. "You'll have to wait to see more," he added, whisking Josh away from the place. "That, my dear Joshua, is true love, perfect love, never ending love! It is God's love, did you feel it?" he asked. Josh fainted, overcome by the spectacular scene he had just witnessed.

"Josh, Josh, wake up! Someone was patting his face, "Wake up Josh!" He opened his eyes and squinted when someone shined a light at him. "Are you okay?" someone asked. "Where am I? What happened?" he asked. "Is he going to be alright, or should we call for an ambulance?" the coach asked. Josh sat up, he felt a little dizzy and nauseated as he sat in the dust, trying to get oriented to his surroundings. "Did I black out? How long was I laying there?" he asked. "It was like two minutes, that's all." He heard someone say. "Really, it seemed a lot longer," he said. "You're going to have a big knot on your head tomorrow! Are you feeling okay Josh? You don't need to go to the emergency room, do you?" the coach asked. "Of course he needs to go! I'll take him in my car," Kayla said as she broke through the crowd.

She knelt down and hugged him. "Help him to my car you guys," she said as she took charge of the situation. She whispered in his ear, "I think your coach would put you back in the game!" "I know he would, I'm alright. I don't need to go to the hospital!" he protested. "OH NO YOU DON'T MISTER, YOU'RE GOING!" she said with authority. "OKAY, okay, I'll go!" he laughed. "I love you!" he said as he fell back in her arms. "We love you too Josh!" The guys on his team teased. "So do we Josh!" yelled some guys from the other team. "We all love you Josh!" the crowd yelled. Someone in the booth heard that and he typed in, "WE LOVE YOU JOSH!" It flashed on the big board. "You see that Josh, we all love you!" Kayla said as she walked next to the big guys who were carrying him. He laughed and thought about what God had just showed him. Under his breath his whispered, "I love you too Jesus!"

Josh was treated and released from the hospital emergency room. Their instructions were to wake him every few hours to check on him. Kayla drove him home and his mom went to pick up his prescription. With three women, his mom, Kayla, and Bethany babying him, he settled into his comfy nest of pillows and blankets, asked for a drink and the remote then drifted off to sleep. After gently kissing his cheek, Cami and the girls tiptoed out of the family room and into the kitchen were they could talk without disturbing him. Kayla's friends were patiently waiting for her in her car so she said her good byes and left. Bethany went upstairs to bed leaving her mother alone in the kitchen. She made herself some tea and got her Bible from the kitchen desk. The room was quiet, except for that darn song that was stuck in her head from the concert, "We all live in a yellow…ahhh!" she cried, "make it stop!" She opened up her Bible and read two of her favorite chapters, Revelation 21-22. It was a description of the New Jerusalem, the city of God. She loved thinking about it because it would be her home someday. "No more pain, no more sorrow, no more separation from the ones we love……" she quietly said. Tears streamed down her cheeks, "I love my family so much……and I miss him" she quietly sobbed. Please be with him," she whispered. She didn't realize it, but Jesus had his hands on her shoulders. He softly whispered into her ear, "I love them too, and I love you…..more than you can imagine." And knowing that she was missing Derek and needing his support and love, he whispered, "I know you're lonely, I see your tears. I'm here for you, don't worry. I know how much you've suffered and worried, just don't give up, don't ever give up hope. I'll take care of everything, you just rest now," he said softly. She sat up straight and looked up. What she had heard took her breath away. "I hear you…….I heard your voice Jesus…..thank you….. I love you!" she whispered. She sat quietly sipping her tea, waiting to hear his voice again.

While Josh slept, he had another dream. This time he and Jesus were in his front yard looking at a fruit tree. Jesus walked to the garage and came back carrying a ladder and the tree trimmers. "What are you going to do Lord?" Josh asked. "I need to trim the dead branches off of your fruit tree." Jesus explained. He climbed up and began trimming. As he worked he talked to Josh about how pruning the tree would produce more and better fruit. "Do you know all the fruit of the Spirit Josh?" he asked. "Um, no I don't know all of them, just love," he said with a grin. Jesus smiled and said, "I'll name them for you then,

"LOVE, JOY, PEACE, PATIENCE, KINDNESS, GOODNESS,

FAITHFULNESS, GENTLENESS, AND SELF CONTROL"

He stood back to examine his work. "Try to keep your tree healthy, if you don't prune it, I will, and that's not going to be very enjoyable for you. It doesn't always feel good to have things cut off, but it's beneficial. The dead branches are the useless things in your life that don't produce anything," he explained. He reached up and pulled off an apple that was brown and shriveled up. "This is bad fruit, not the kind I expect you to grow." Then he pulled off a beautiful, ripe apple and said, "Now this is the kind of fruit you will get if you'll do what I tell you. Stay close to me, I'll teach you everything you need to know about growing good fruit, like love." He picked up a large pile of branches and headed for the burn pile in the backyard. Josh collected a whole basket of the apples. "Hey, Jesus," he called out, "want to help me bake a pie for Kayla?" "You mean you want to make her a "love" pie?" he asked with a big grin on his face. "Yeah," Josh blushed, "I think I do love her," he chuckled. "And remember what you told me, love is a verb. Well, making her a pie is an action, right?" he laughed. "That's right, so is helping me with these sticks!" Jesus laughed. "You wanna show some love by bringing the rest out back, please?"

As they watched the branches burn, they talked. "Let me tell you, no, let me show you something else about your fruit tree." Jesus said. Josh followed him to the front yard and watched in utter amazement as he approached the tree, put his arms around it and gently pulled it out of the ground, as if it were a small weed. "Superman" he said under his breath. Jesus just smiled. He laid the tree down and examined the roots. "I want you to be like a tree… and leave! Just kidding, I want you to be like a tree with deep roots. Your roots will go deep when you meditate on the word day and night. You'll be strong and the winds of life won't be able to blow you over. I am the Word and out of me flow springs of Living Water. Plant your tree next to me and it will grow tall, strong and healthy. And, you'll have the best fruit you've ever tasted growing all over you!" Josh pictured himself as a fruity tree and laughed. Jesus picked up the basket of "love", "Let's make that pie now, or shall we make two?" he asked.

17

⚬⚬⚬

The Fishing Boat

Cami woke Josh at 2:00 in the morning. "Are you okay honey?" she asked. "Mom, I'm alright, you don't need to keep waking me up!" he growled. "I'm just following the doctor's orders, now go back to sleep," she whispered sweetly as she tucked him in. He was on the sofa in the family room and she would sleep nearby on the cushy recliner. She set the clock for 5:00 then turned the light off. In less than a minute he was sound asleep again.

He was back in the front yard with Jesus. "Hey Josh, would you put the ladder and trimmers away?" Jesus asked. "Sure, thanks again for pruning my tree." When he walked back from the garage, Jesus was standing on the curb looking at a fishing boat and trailer that was parked in front of his house. He ran up to Jesus and asked excitedly, "Is this our boat? I love to fish!" "It's our boat Josh, but I'm not taking you fishing for fish, I'm going to make you a fisher of men!" Jesus said with a big smile on his face. "What, what do you mean?" Josh sounded disappointed. "Oh now Josh, don't be that way. Let me show you what I mean, hop in the boat." Jesus said. Josh got in the boat as he had instructed. "Close your eyes and listen, what do you hear?" Jesus asked. Josh listened for a moment. "I think I hear seagulls," he said as he opened his eyes. It delighted him to find himself in an old wooden fishing boat along with a bunch of grubby, sweaty fishermen wearing dress-like clothing. Jesus stood up and introduced his friends to Josh.

"Josh, this is James and John, over there is Andrew, Phillip and Thomas. And this is Matthew and the big hairy one holding the net is Peter!" Jesus laughed then he introduced the others. "Wow, it's your followers, your crew!" "They're my "home boys" from Galilee." Jesus laughed, he obviously enjoyed being with his old friends.

"Take us out Peter!" Jesus said. "Josh talked to the men about Jesus as a gentle wind blew them far away from the shore. They told him stories about how Jesus had fed over fifteen thousand people with one little boy's lunch and how he had healed so many sick and lame people. "He's the messiah, you know?" John whispered. "I know he is John, I have no doubt about that!" Josh responded. "Well, he may be, but I still need more proof of that." Thomas whispered. "What more do you need to see?" asked Matthew in an angry tone, "he has shown us so many signs already!" Just then a strong wind blew into the sails and made the waves grow larger. "A storm now approaches, take down the sails!" Peter commanded. The men worked quickly to do as he said. Meanwhile, Jesus fell asleep in the back of the boat. Josh watched him as he slept, amazed that the wind didn't wake him. He was under a small covering when the strong rain began to fall but he didn't seem to hear it or feel it. "He must be exhausted." Josh said. "He walks all day, everybody wants to see him," James said, "and his miracles," he added.

Josh began to panic as the water crashed over the sides of the boat. "We're going to sink! Jesus, wake up and do something!" he cried out. "No Josh, don't wake him just yet, he's tired." Peter said sternly "We've been through this before my friend and we trust that Yeshua can calm the storm." "We're in no danger young man. Trust me when I tell you that our sleeping friend will save us!" Matthew said calmly. "Don't be afraid, he doesn't like us to be afraid. He wants us to trust completely in him." James said looking at the sleeping Son of God. Joshua sat down and waited with the fishermen. He looked around at the men that Jesus had chosen to be his followers. He wondered if they realized what an impact they would have on the world with their testimonies of having been so close to God's only Son and having learned directly from him. He was sure they didn't know yet about the Father's plan to sacrifice his Son to pay for the sins of the world. They didn't yet know that Jesus was the King of all kings and Lord of all lords.

He shook his head and smiled about what he had just read in the book of Revelation. He read that God would one day honor these men by naming the twelve foundation layers of the New Jerusalem after them, all except Judas of course. Or was it was the twelve gates made of pearl that would bear their names, he forgot which. Not long after, Jesus woke up. He sat up and stretched. "Good, you are all waiting for me. I am pleased with your faith!" he said loudly. They all smiled and looked at each other as if to congratulate themselves for trusting in him. He stood up, the wind blew his hair back and the pouring rain soaked his clothes. He turned his head to smile at the men then he gave a wink to Josh as he held out his arms and shouted, "Peace, be still!"

With that mighty command, the wind stopped, the dark clouds rolled away and the sea settled to a peaceful calm. The late afternoon sun peeked out and rays of golden warmth filled the sky. Josh sat in awe of the God-man. He felt such peace and fulfillment being with him. The men talked and laughed for a while as the water from the sea gently rocked the old boat. Then Peter stood up, clapped his large, rough hands together and said in a loud voice, "Enough of this talking, the night is nearly here! Grab that net young man, there's fish to be caught!" Jesus looked at Josh, shrugged his shoulders and said, "You heard him, let's catch some fish!"

"Honey, wake up, Josh, wake up! Kayla is here to have breakfast with us. Joshua, are you okay?" his mother asked as she gently shook him. "Huh, what time is it?" he asked, his eyes squinting in the lamplight. Kayla's here, she brought you something to eat, so get up!" she said. He stumbled into the kitchen, "Hi Kayla, you're up early," he said as he scratched his chin stubble. "So are you!" she laughed, knowing he got up because of her. "How are you feeling this morning?" she asked in a happy, sunny voice, and feeling unusually at home with his family, like she fit right in. "You two sit down," she said, "I'll get the breakfast for you." She set the table with four flower print paper plates and napkins. "Is Bethany eating with us?" she asked. "I'll go get her right now!" Cami replied, happy to help in any way she could. Kayla pulled a hot dish out of her quilted bag, "Hope you like breakfast casserole Josh," she said, "and I made you some homemade biscuits." She proudly sat the warm food on the table. "I even brought a jar of my homemade strawberry jam, you have to try some!" "Wow, did you stay up all night?" he asked as he suddenly started feeling very hungry. "Well, I couldn't sleep, so I went shopping for the stuff to make all of this for you, hope you'll like it," she giggled. "It smells great, thank you!" he said. "I can't wait to try it!" Kayla poured orange juice for everyone then Cami said the blessing.

The four of them had a nice conversation as they enjoyed their breakfast. "This was so thoughtful of you Kayla, thank you! And you're such a good cook for being so young!" Cami said as she cleared the table. "Oh, thank you, I'm glad you liked it!" Kayla said as she helped clear the dishes from the table. "My bus will be here soon. It was nice to meet you Kayla. Maybe we can do it again soon, I mean, you don't have to cook for us or anything, I meant we can have you over again, that'd be cool!" Bethany said as she grabbed her backpack and headed for the door. "I'd like that Bethany, see you later. Have a great day at school!" Kayla said. "She's sweet, I like her," she said. "Oh, you can't mean Bethany! She's a spoiled brat, right mom?" Josh teased. "No, that'd be you. You're the brat around here!" Cami laughed.

"Knock-knock" "Good morning, I hope you don't mind if I come to the back door. I saw Bethany and she said you were all in the kitchen." It was Pastor Dan. "I heard that Josh had a little accident last night?" he said. "Oh hi, come in pastor!" Cami said, delighted to see him. She shook his hand and pulled him inside. "Yes, he has quite a bump on his forehead," she said. The three of them gathered around Josh to examine his bump. "Does it hurt when I touch it honey?" She asked as she pushed on it gently. "Ouch, yes that hurts!" he laughed. "Hi Pastor Dan, thanks for coming to check on me," Josh said as he shook the pastor's hand. "Sit down Pastor Dan, would you like some breakfast? Kayla made it, it's really good!" Cami asked. "Sure, I never say no to good food!" he laughed. While he ate his meal, the others had coffee. They enjoyed his company, he seemed like a regular guy and Josh really liked him. "Hey Pastor Dan, do you know anything about cars? I need to put a new starter in mine." Josh asked. "Well, maybe I can help you, I've had to do a lot of work on my old car, so I kind of know what I'm doing." he said. "Great, thanks Pastor! I'll get dressed and be right down!" Josh kissed his mom's cheek then he kissed Kayla's before running upstairs. "Slow down Josh, you're going to get dizzy!" his mother warned. "It's so nice of you to offer to help him!" she said. "I try to make Fridays my day to help people fix things. Just don't tell Miriam, she'll want me to install that ceiling fan I've been avoiding!" he laughed. "Thanks for the great breakfast Kayla, you're a good cook!" he said. "Oh thank you Pastor Dan," she blushed. "You're welcome to visit us at church anytime Kayla, we'd love to have you there, especially on pot-luck days!" he laughed. She laughed too, thinking that he was really funny and nice, she liked him. After the kitchen was cleaned up, she packed up her things and left for work at the horse ranch. "She's a keeper Josh!" his mother told him. "Amen to that!" the Pastor concurred. Josh just smiled and pictured himself back on his fishing boat reeling in a beautiful mermaid named Kayla, without a hook of course.

While Pastor Dan and Josh were outside with their heads under the hood of Josh's car, a loud pickup truck pulled into the driveway. It was Kyle! "Hey Kyle, it's good to see you out of the hospital! How are you feeling?" Josh said as he wiped the grease from his hands and walked over to hug his friend. "I'm doing great! I feel as good as new!" Pastor Dan walked up to Kyle and said, "Hey buddy, I'm glad to see you walking around!" "Thanks Pastor, and thanks for coming to see me and for praying for me!" Kyle said. "God is watching over you Kyle, there's a reason you're still here," the Pastor said. Kyle smiled at that comment. "Hope I don't let him down," he said.

The three of them went over to the car and Josh told Kyle what they were working on. "I can help you too, I've got nothing else going on today," Kyle said. "Hey Josh, what's this I hear about you getting knocked in the head by a baseball, I thought baseball was so safe?" he asked sarcastically. "Ah, he was just jealous of you getting all the attention, right Josh?" Pastor laughed. "Yeah, right, I'm sick of him getting all those cute nurses to pamper him and wait on him!" Josh teased. "If you want that treatment, you'll need more than a bump on the head you'll need real man's injury, like mine!" Kyle bragged. "Hey Pastor, speaking of injuries, I hear you fell off the roof of your house and broke your legs up really bad?" Josh asked. "Yep, now that was a real man's injury! I was adjusting the antenna so I could watch the football game more clearly," he bragged. "Oh yeah, football, a real man's game!" They grunted and then they laughed.

"I saw this big gash on Peter's arm. He must have gotten it while he was out fishing," Josh said. "Peter who?" they asked. "Ah man, I'm getting my dreams and real life mixed up! I had a dream that I was on the fishing boat with Jesus and his disciples. It was so amazing, I got to see Jesus calm the storm!" he said. "Really, that's awesome Josh! I've never had a dream like that!" Pastor Dan said. "I've had the coolest dreams all week and Jesus is in all of them! He's taught me so much and I feel like I really know him now. We go on all sorts of adventures together. I just love having these dreams, I hope they never end!" he said excitedly. He was glad he had someone to talk to about his dreams, someone who understood and felt the same way. "I'd love to hear all about these dreams. Try to write down the details so you don't forget, okay?" Pastor said. "God is doing something special with you Josh!" "I wish you could have one of these dreams Pastor," Josh said. "Bring it on Jesus!" Pastor Dan said loudly as he looked to the sky.

After they finished with Josh's car, Pastor Dan left for home. Kyle asked Josh about taking Kayla and Dakota out to eat and maybe to see a movie later. "Are you sure you're up to that already, you just got out of the hospital?" Josh asked. "I actually feel fine, a little sore, but fine. You should talk, with that big knot on your head!" Kyle laughed. Josh told him that Dakota was his boss's daughter and that he had seen her when he went to dinner at their house. He was surprised that Joe would let her go out after what had happened with Mike. Kyle explained to him that Joe wasn't real comfortable with it until he had heard that Josh and his girlfriend were going along. "You told him that before you asked me? Dude…. what were you thinking?" Josh asked. "I knew I could count on you to go. Besides when Dakota told her dad that it was you going with us, he was relieved. He told her that he trusted you, why, I don't know!" Kyle smiled. Josh called to ask Kayla if she could go, she said yes. They planned to meet Kyle and Dakota at the restaurant at 6:00. Josh didn't ask if Kyle knew about Dakota being pregnant, he couldn't find the words. He thought he should wait awhile before he hit him with that news. Besides, she should be the one to tell him. He also hoped it wouldn't be awkward to see Dakota after the way he flirted with her the other night.

After Kyle left, Josh wanted to try out the car. Remembering what Jesus had said in one of his dreams about meeting someone down by the lake, he drove down there to see if it might be true and who he was to meet. He parked the car and got out to walk. There were people everywhere, how would he know who it was? Then he felt an urge to turn and walk in the other direction. He saw a kid in the distance sitting on the back of a park bench. As he got closer, he recognized the hooded sweatshirt and hat that the boy was wearing. "It's one of those creeps that attacked us!" he said. Before he went any closer, he looked all around the area. Not seeing the others, he ran up to the boy.

"Hey you, I want my ring back!" he said harshly. "What are talking about, I don't know you man!" was the snarky remark the boy made. Josh came around and got in the boy's face. "YOU DO KNOW ME PUNK, AND IF YOU DON'T GIVE ME MY RING, I'LL CALL THE COPS ON YOU!" he threatened. He calmed himself down a bit and asked the boy where he lived. "I AIN'T GOTTA TELL YOU NOTHIN!" The boy said as he started walking away. Josh knew there were only a handful of black families that lived in town. "You look a lot like Riley, but there's no way your related to him! Riley and Jasmine are too nice to be related to someone like you!" Josh said, rather hatefully. "Who do you think you are talking about my grandparents like you know them, you don't know them!" the boy said. "Are you kidding me? You're their grandson?" Josh sounded astonished. "You're not from around here, are you?" he asked. "I'm from Chicago, not this stupid little town. This place makes me sick!" the boy said. Josh was slightly offended by that remark, but didn't respond to it. "I'm going to follow you home and tell your grandparents what you did. Where are those other guys you were with?" he asked. "They don't live here and you ain't going to tell my family nothing! I don't have any ring of yours, so leave me alone!" the boy snarled.

Josh calmed himself again and said, "Look, I'm sorry I called you a punk, I just want my ring back. I like your grandparents, everybody here likes them and I don't want to cause them any trouble, but they need to know the kind of kids you hang out with. I didn't see you doing what the other two did and I know you weren't the one who stole the money and my ring. I'll tell your grandparents that, if you'll get my ring back for me, okay?" he asked. The boy thought about it and then said he would get the ring back for him. Josh thanked him and turned to walk away. "I know where your grandparents live, I'll be there in the morning!" he yelled, not turning around to see the boy's reaction.

Later, when he was getting ready for his date, he looked in the mirror to examine his bump and he thought about what he would do if anyone were to jump out at them that night. He practiced what his reaction might be, "What you looking at punk? You better run, I'll kick...," he stopped and laughed at himself, "*I can't believe what I said to those guys, they must have laughed all the way home,*" he thought. "*What a loser, that was so lame!*" "*You're not a loser Josh, I told you to use my word, remember? When they ran away, they weren't laughing!*" he heard the Spirit say. "*Maybe they saw Gabe standing behind me?*" he thought. "*Yeah it was Gabe alright, and five of his angel buddies standing with him!*" the Spirit said.

"Really, that's awesome! Then I don't have to worry about a thing!" he said confidently as he pulled a ball cap over his bump. "Fishers of men, that's right! I've got my angels and we're going to catch you!" he said, pointing at the mirror but thinking about the kid at the park. He pretended to reel in a big fish while talking to himself in his "country boy" voice, he said, "Will ya look at that, I done caught me a big mouthed..... bass! He laughed at himself and said, "you're weird, but handsome!"

His dream and all of that talk about fishing got him thinking about his dad again. He sat down at his desk and opened one of the side drawers. After looking through the papers, and assorted junk, he found what he was looking for. It was a picture of him and his dad on the bank of their favorite Canadian lake, holding the biggest fish he had ever caught in his life. It was a Northern Pike and it had to have weighed more than he did at the time. He was nine years old when his dad, his brother, his two uncles and their sons went on their annual fishing trip. It was only Josh's second time going with "the guys" and he absolutely loved every minute of it. Even the rainy days were fun, the older guys played cards while the boys listened to all of their "fish tales" from previous trips. They always rented a cabin and two or three fishing boats. The lake was huge so they needed to hire local guides to navigate the confusing landscape and lead them to the best spots.

Josh sat back in his chair and got lost in his memories, he smiled as he tried to remember all of the wonderful times he had on that particular fishing trip. The first thing he remembered was waking up before the sun rise and the smell of the bacon and eggs his mom made for breakfast. He and Caleb helped load up the truck, he recalled carefully placing his brand new fishing rod next to theirs. They met up with the others at the bait and tackle shop where all the fishermen loved to congregate. Then they would stop for a candy bar and chips at the gas station, the boys were instructed to use the bathroom while the men filled up the gas tanks. He felt proud that his dad always led the convoy of vehicles all the way to Canada.

Then he thought about being in the boat with his dad and brother, he loved watching his dad bait the hooks and cast the lines out into the deep water. The scenery was so beautiful, not a sign of civilization anywhere. It was quiet, no one talked unless they had a fish on their line, then everyone whooped it up, well, not everyone, the guys in the other boats got busy, not wanting to be out fished. He always enjoyed watching and waiting for a tug on his line, at that time it was the best feeling in the world to him. The water was crystal clear and he liked to lean his head over the boat and look at the big boulders way down on the bottom of the lake. The guides would jump out of the boats and onto the big, flat rocks and pull the boats up. Then they would prepare a shore lunch of freshly caught walleye, beans and fried potatoes, he could almost taste it now, fish always tasted better when it was cooked over a campfire. Afterward, when they were done fishing, he and his cousins would go swimming (or maybe it was only wading) in the icy water near the cabin. What fun they had together.

Now they were all grown up. Some of them had gotten married and had already started a family and couple of them went off to college, his brother joined the Navy and his oldest cousin had moved to Alaska. He worked on, of all things, a fishing boat! Josh smiled as he thought about all of them, *"I wonder if any of them are Christians? I doubt it, well, maybe some of them, who knows? I should try to get in touch with them, see what they're up to. It'd be cool to go to Alaska and visit Wally...maybe someday,"* he sighed. He slipped the photo back into the drawer, then finished getting ready.

18

⊶∞⊷

The Sidewalk

Kayla didn't want Josh to drive so she picked him up and drove to the restaurant. She, being more practical thought he should stay home in bed. But he, being more stubborn won the argument. When they got there they waited outside for Kyle and Dakota. They sat on a bench under a tree and talked. She mentioned her senior prom again and this time Josh had to respond. He wasn't too thrilled about going to a high school prom, but knowing how important it was her he decided to ask if he could escort her to it. The wise words of Joe were marching through his mind, "Happy wife- happy life." Even though she wasn't his wife yet, he wanted to please her. She then asked him if he were ready to meet her family, to which he replied, "Of course, I'd love to meet them!" He had just score two major points with her.

A few minutes later, Kyle and Dakota pulled into the parking lot. Kyle's truck was so loud that Josh and Kayla heard it long before they saw it. As they made their way inside, Kyle made sure that Josh saw him holding the door for the girls. Josh nodded his approval, happy to see that he had taken his advice. He always liked coming to this particular restaurant because the food was always good and the servers were friendly and fast but what he really liked about it was the atmosphere. It was a gigantic old barn that had been converted into an Italian villa complete with cobblestone floors. There were real candles on the old wooden tables, and there were real flowers and trees growing inside. It had large windows on two sides and ceiling windows though which they could see the stars and the moon at night. Murals of beautiful Italian landscapes had been painted on the other large walls which added to the character and beauty to the place.

The four of them had a great time once they got past the introductions and small talk. Kyle's eyes seemed to sparkle whenever he looked at Dakota, and it was the same with her. *"They look so good together."* Josh thought, *"I wonder if Kayla and I look that good when we're together?"* He didn't know it but the other three were thinking the same thing. When the food was served they all began eating. Josh heard the voice of the Holy Spirit deep inside his heart reminding him to give thanks for the food. He decided to ignore the urge to pray in front of his friends, even if it was making him feel a little guilty. *"I promise to thank you the next time,"* he thought." *"Are you ashamed of me?"* he heard his friend ask. "Um, would you guys mind if I say a little prayer?" he asked. No one objected. He bowed his head and quietly said, "Thank you for this food and for my friends." "AMEN" they all said rather loudly. *"I am so pleased with you for acknowledging me,"* Jesus said. Josh just smiled at everyone and said, "Let's dig in!"

After they had finished their dinner, they decided to play a game of mini golf. It wasn't far so they decided to walk. As Josh and Kayla walked arm in arm, she kept a look out for anyone who looked suspicious, while he walked with confidence, knowing that he had a group of large angels following him. He hadn't told her about his invisible escorts so she marveled at his lack of fear. They all had fun playing golf. The two girls laughed hysterically as Josh and Kyle showed off their goofy side. They could be hilarious at times, but sometimes they were just plain annoying.

Kyle was starting to feel some pain in his chest. It was hard for him to hit the ball one handed while trying not to overdo his swing. His mom had warned him not to go out so soon. Josh's mom had said the same thing to him but he and Kyle were dead set on going. Then Dakota started feeling a little nauseated and light headed. Her parents also thought it wasn't a good idea for her to go out, but then they decided that it might be good for her to have a little fun. She seemed to be punishing herself for what she had done by staying home all the time. None of the three had said anything about how they felt because they were having such a good time. Kayla seemed to know that they weren't feeling well and suggested that they call it a night and go home, but they wouldn't hear of it, no one wanted to go home, not yet anyway.

After the game they walked a little further down the lighted walkway to the ice cream stand. The place was busy. Josh saw that it looked safe with all the families and sports teams hanging around. Although, he did see some teenagers standing off to the side. He imagined that from now on he would always be checking his surroundings for trouble. Music played from the speakers and the lights were bright around the little shop. Most of the people seemed to be having a good time enjoying the warm evening while some in the crowd seemed to be up to mischief. The mood that night was festive and light, while at the same time, dark and foreboding.

Josh spied a group of kids dressed all in black with tattoos and piercings everywhere. They wore shirts with demonic creatures and symbols on them. He didn't like that look at all, it gave him the creeps. He knew some of those girls were into witchcraft and stuff like that and the guys played some really dark video games, games that he never got into. It was rumored that this bunch met at the old house on Cedarville Road to practice occult rituals. Music came over the loud speaker that made him feel uneasy and he began to sense that something evil was lurking around the place. Then he saw her, it was his little sister Bethany. She was hanging out with some tall, dark creep! Josh watched in horror as she lit up a cigarette or something. He quickly turned away so she wouldn't see him. Not knowing what to do, he guided his friends around the corner to a table where they could sit. He and Kyle went around to the front to order the ice cream.

"Kyle, look over there, that's Bethany!" he said as he pointed her out. Kyle saw her and thought the same thing he did, "I'll kill that kid if he hurts her!" he growled. "What should I do? I don't want to make her mad by embarrassing her. But look at that guy, he's definitely not her type, what's she doing with him?" Josh fumed. "We gotta do something!" Kyle said smacking his fist on his hand then flinching from the pain it caused him. He was like a big brother to Bethany, he'd known her most of his life.

Josh turned to look at her and saw her looking right at him. She approached him and Kyle with her friend at her side. "What are you guys doing here?" she laughed. "Hey, this is my friend Charles," she said as she looked Josh right in the eyes. "This is my brother Josh and my friend Kyle." The three boys stood there like statues and grunted a hello to each other. "You need a ride home?" Josh asked his sister. "Nah, Charles's friend can drop me off," she said. "Make it soon!" he snarled. "What's your problem?" she snarled back. He ignored her remark and walked away. He ordered the ice cream and went over to sit with his own friends. Kayla and Dakota noticed the change in their mood and asked why they were so quiet. Josh told them about Bethany and who she was with. Kayla looked around and spotted Bethany and Charles and gave them a friendly wave.

"Don't encourage her Kayla! I don't want her to think I'm okay with her seeing that guy!" he said. Kayla poked him and said, "Haven't you ever heard that you shouldn't judge a book by its cover?" He immediately thought of the two boxes in his storage closet. "That's CJ, he's a junior at my school. I happen to know that he is really smart, like a rocket scientist smart!" she said. "Shut up! Are you serious?" he laughed. "That's what all the teachers say." she responded. "Well, he looks like a vampire to me. Why do they dress like that, with all the skulls and demon stuff?" he wondered. "I don't know, but they're pretty harmless, they do more damage to themselves than to others," she said. "Sounds depressing, hope Bethany isn't like that," Kyle added. Dakota needed to get home, Josh's headache was getting worse, and Kyle was really in pain, so they left. Kayla thanked Josh for the fun date and he thanked her for the ride. They kissed and said goodnight.

Somehow Bethany got home before he did. "Don't tell mom, please!" she begged. He took her by the arm and pulled her into the kitchen. "What are thinking? I don't want you seeing that guy again, do you hear me?" he said sternly. "Don't worry about it, you're not in charge of my life anymore!" she said. He tried to calm down. "Look, I'm sorry. I just don't want anything to happen to you, and I don't like the looks of that kid," he said. "Kid, he's only two years younger than you!" her voice softened. Then she assured him that she would let him talk to Charles before she went out with him again.

"Does mom know about him?" he asked. "She's too busy with her own life to care about mine," she responded. Josh found himself defending his mother, "She cares about you Bethany, she's just got a lot on her mind. And this thing with dad has had her really stressed out. I hear her crying at night, don't you?" he asked. "I guess so. But I've got junk happening too! All those, she paused, never mind!" She caught herself before revealing too much to him. "What's going on with you? I'm worried about you!" he said. "There's nothing you can do about it, so don't worry about it," she said. Then she went upstairs and closed the door behind her.

Cami was in her room watching some Christian program. Josh said good night to her through the door, then he opened it a crack and said, "Mom, why don't you check on Bethany, I think something is bothering her." She slipped on her robe and went to Bethany's room. She knocked on door and peeked in and of course, Bethany had her laptop open and had her headphones on. Cami got her attention, "Want to talk honey?" she asked. "No, I'm good," Bethany responded. "Well, is everything alright? You can tell me if something is bothering you." Cami said. "No, I'm fine, good night," she smiled at her mom then went right back to whatever she was doing. Cami let out a loud sigh and said, "Alright then honey, good night, I love you!" "Love you too," Bethany said without looking up. It was very frustrating for Cami, she didn't know how to break through to her. She went back to her room and talked to Jesus about it. Then she got to feeling lonely again, she missed her husband, she missed her son Caleb and she missed Bethany. Then she realized how close her and Josh had become over the past few days. She took a deep breath and smiled, trusting that God was able to work all things out for the good. As she lay back on her pillows, she dozed off and began to dream, but that's another story.

Josh went to bed after he took something for his headache, which was also something that helped him sleep. He was in too much pain to think about anything so he just got comfortable and in no time he was out. He was dreaming about his house again. This time he and

Jesus were out in the front yard playing catch with a football. Then down the sidewalk came a guy who looked just like Charles riding on a skateboard. He stopped near them to ask for directions.

"Hey dudes, can you tell me how to get to Heaven, I'm kind of lost," he asked. "Josh walked right up to him a said as he pointed to Jesus, "He's the way. He's the only way to get to Heaven." Jesus strode up to the boy and shook his hand. "Hi, I'm the Way, the Truth and the Life." The young man said, "Hi, my name is Rage."

Jesus smiled and thought of a verse, which he quoted: But I know where you stay and when you come and go and how you "Rage" against me, 2 Kings 19:27. Rage took a step back and said, "Whoa, my name's in the Bible, that's totally rad, man!" "I totally agree!" Jesus said. Josh just rolled his eyes at the two of them, thinking what a strange pair they made. "He can't possibly want to be friends with this guy," he said to himself. "Oh, I've got another verse for you," Jesus said. "Jesus, can I talk to you for a second?" Josh interrupted. "Excuse us Rage, I'll be right back," Jesus said as he followed Josh. "This guy's not exactly the type of person you should hang around with. I think he's a Satan worshipper!" Josh whispered. Jesus threw his head back and roared with laughter. "Joshua, Joshua, all of you have sinned and come short of my glory. Every last one of you needs salvation, there's no one who's worthy or good enough to enter Heaven, "he said, lightly slapping him on the back, "that's where I come in, you are made righteous and worthy through me. Remember what you told him, "I am the Way" so I think I can handle one little Devil worshiper, don't you? And Josh, don't be jealous, your name is in the Bible too!" he added.

Just then a loud, rusty old car squealed up to the curb next to them. "THERE YOU ARE! I've been looking everywhere for you! Get in this car, NOW!" the angry woman yelled. "I better go before she **really** gets mad!" Rage said before hopping into the car. As the noisy car sped away, Jesus yelled out, "Come back any time, we'd love to talk to you!" "What do you mean *"we"?* You may like him, but I don't want people like that in my house!" Josh protested. "He needs a good friend, and I'd like that friend to be you." Jesus said as he patted Josh's shoulder. "Ah man," Josh huffed, "I sure hope that doesn't include his psycho mom!" They both laughed. "It does!" Jesus laughed again.

"Go long Josh!" Jesus yelled as he faded back. He threw the football high, so high that Josh had to jump for it. He caught it then threw it right back. He turned and spotted a young girl riding her bike down the sidewalk toward him. She stopped her bike next to him and asked if he had seen her kitten. She described the kitten as being black with white feet and she called him Mr. Puffy. He told her that he hadn't seen the kitten but he would help her look for it. She thanked him and told him that her name was Kristina.

Then the dream changed scenes. He and Kristina were calling out for Mr. Puffy as they walked along the sidewalk, then the sidewalk became a dirt path that cut through a field of long yellow grass. Alongside of the path he saw a dusty dirt road that had lots of deep ruts and large pot holes. "Where are we Josh?" Kristina asked. "I'm not sure, but uh, I think we may be in Africa, look over there!" he said, pointing to some trees in the distance and the giraffes that were eating the leaves from them. "Look Kristina, there's a herd of zebras, aren't they magnificent?!" he exclaimed. "This must be the Serengeti, I think we're in Tanzania!" he said excitedly. "I did a report on this place when I was in school!" They both turned back to see a muddy vehicle bouncing along the road. It pulled up next to them and stopped. "Hello my friends," the friendly man said. "Would you like a ride to the village?" he asked. "Thank you, we would like that!" Josh said, happy to see some other humans.

"My name is Joshua and my little friend here is Kristina, we're from America," he said. "Welcome to Africa, my name is Juma, this is my wife Ada and our Swedish friend in the back is Johanna." Juma asked Josh what they were doing in Tanzania, "Are you going on a lion safari?" "More like a kitten safari! Kristina lost her little Mr. Fluffy." Josh explained. "It's Mr. Puffy Josh!" Kristina said smiling up at him with an adorable, toothless grin. They drove over the bumpy road a little faster than Josh would have liked to, pulling over twice to watch the hippos in the river and once to retrieve Kristina's hat. After a long, hot, bumpy ride, Juma pulled into the shaded village and parked next to two other muddy vehicles. "Oh good, Pastor Dan and his lovely wife Miriam are here!" he said as he hopped out. "What, did you say Pastor Dan is here?" Josh was astonished. "Yes, Miriam is going to teach some Bible classes to the children and Pastor Dan is helping us fix some things. He will be preaching later tonight, you are welcome to join us," Juma said. Pastor Dan was wiping the dirt off his hands as he walked up to the vehicle. "Hey Josh, it's nice seeing you here!" It all seemed perfectly natural to the Pastor to see Josh in Africa. "Well, well, well, what are you doing here Pastor?" Josh asked. "Well, well, WELL!" The Pastor laughed and pointed to the large drilling truck. "I helped them drill a well today! It is my day to fix things, remember?"

They all walked back to the village talking along the way. "I lived in Liberia for a while when I was a kid, my parents were missionaries there," the Pastor said. "This is our first time in this part of Africa," he added. "It's our first time here too," Josh said smiling down at Kristina. Miriam joined them and Pastor Dan put his arm around her waist as they walked to the main building. "My wife was actually born in the jungles of Brazil. Her parents were missionaries too," he said. "That's cool! I'd like to hear more about that sometime," Josh said. They washed up in the clean water that came from the well then they joined the others at the large wooden table. Pastor Dan said the blessing then the women of the village brought out platters of food for them to eat and pure well water for them to drink. Josh looked around for Kristina but couldn't find her anywhere. Soon everyone got up and started searching for her. Then he spotted her down by the river. He ran to get her after hearing that the river was full of large crocodiles. "Kristina, come here honey, get away from the water!" he called out as he ran toward her. Then he suddenly stopped and froze in his tracks. What he saw frightened him so much, he was afraid to move.

It was a pride of lions moving in on the little girl. A large male lion was crouching low to the ground as he slowly inched toward her. Josh watched helplessly as Kristina bent over to pick something up. It was Mr. Puffy! He motioned to her not to move and to be quiet. Little did he know that the whole village was standing right behind him collectively holding their breath with him, suddenly out of nowhere another male lion appeared. He ran past Kristina and pounced on the crouching lion. The battle was fierce! The two huge cats used their strong paws and sharp teeth as they tried to overpower each other. Meanwhile, Kristina and Mr. Puffy ran with the others to a safe spot in the middle of the village. Josh knelt down, closed his eyes and hugged his little friend and her kitty. "Oh Kristina, I'm so glad you're okay!" he cried. The Swedish woman tapped Josh on the shoulder and said, "You have some visitors Joshua."

Josh stood up and turned around. To his horror he saw three large lions standing in front of him bearing their fangs and growling at him. Fear gripped him. He and the others backed slowly away as the lions stepped closer and closer to them, licking their lips with hunger. This reminded him of the bible story he had heard as a child about Daniel in the lion's den. "Help me Jesus!" he whispered.

Some of the men from the village threw a heavy net over the lions. The men jumped back when the lions roared loudly and swiped at them with their big claws. Angry at being captured, the lions turned on each other and fought, getting themselves tangled up even more. It was frightening to watch the huge cats fighting and thrashing around on the floor as they tried to escape. Even the sound they made was terrifying. The possibility of one of them getting free from the net made most of the people run away in fear, only a few brave ones stayed to watch. It took a long time for the lions to wear themselves out. They sat down and panted heavily, exhausted from the struggle. Then to the amazement of everyone watching, the three lions began to change into three young men. Josh immediately recognized them. It was the three boys from the park! He stood there not knowing what to do or say.

Jesus broke through the crowd and walked up to Josh. "What do we have here?" He asked. "These are the boys that attacked Kayla and I in the park! That one stole my ring!" Josh said as he pointed at the guilty one. All eyes were on Jesus as he circled around the boys. Then he walked over to Josh again and asked, "Have you ever stolen anything? Have you ever hurt or frightened anyone?" he asked. Josh frowned and didn't say a word knowing that he had also been guilty of those things. Jesus opened his hands to show Josh the nail scars. Then he said, "You see them as predators that need to be captured and punished. I see three frustrated and angry young men caught in the trap of sin. He grabbed the net and flung it aside. "I came to set them free!"

"The Spirit of the Sovereign Lord is upon me, because he has anointed me to preach good news to the poor. He has sent me to proclaim freedom for the prisoners and recovery of sight for the blind, to release the oppressed, to proclaim the year of the Lord's favor."
Jesus
Matthew 4:18-19 NIV

19

⎯⎯⎯◦∞◦⎯⎯⎯

The Angel on the Roof

Josh woke up and realized that the lion dream was a message from God and he knew that God wanted him to do something about it. Since he didn't have to work that morning he decided to pay a visit to his friends, Riley and Jasmine, the grandparents of the boy he had met in the park. They lived in a nice little house on the east side of town. Josh had met Jasmine years ago. She worked at the retirement home his great grandmother had lived in toward the end of her life. He remembered hearing Jasmine talk to his grandma about her (Jasmine's), dream of opening a bakery downtown. Josh always enjoyed his weekly visits with his grandma because he got to sample Jasmine's baked goods while listening to the stories his grandma would tell, mostly stories about his dad. When his grandma died she left Jasmine a thousand dollars to put toward the bakery. Over the years, the two women had become close friends. Jasmine was so overwhelmed by her friend's death and the gift she had given to her that she cried for a week! She determined to honor her friend by naming her sugar cookies after her. She would call them "Sweet Wanda cookies". The thousand dollars was put in the bank and she had added to it over the years. Now she was so excited because she almost had enough to start up her bakery which she planned to name, "The Sweet Life".

Josh was eight years old when he met Jasmine's husband Riley. They met at the grocery store where Riley had worked. He was a nice man and all the customers liked him. It was his custom to wear funny hats to work and hand out stickers to all the children. So because of that he became very popular with the little ones, especially little Joshua. Riley would always let little Josh help bag up the groceries for his mom. Then he would reward him with a sticker, a pat on the head and a piece of candy. That's why the two of them hit it off so well.

Jasmine and Riley both liked Joshua so much that they began treating him like they would their own grandson and he in return treated them like his own grandparents. Their children and grandchildren lived far away and they rarely got to see them. So one day Riley decided to ask permission to take Joshua fishing. The two of them went fishing together many times after that. Almost every Saturday morning for three summers, Riley would show up at Josh's door with a can of worms, two fishing poles and a picnic lunch that Jasmine had made for them. But as Josh grew older, he developed other interests and friends so the fishing dates with Riley slowly faded into fond memories from his childhood. Josh sometimes felt sad that it had ended.

Jasmine and Riley were active members of a little church on Elm Street. They both sang in the choir, Riley mowed the church lawn every week and Jasmine taught the woman's Bible study every other Saturday. Their two grown children, Pearl and Raymond, had families of their own. Raymond had four children and Pearl had one, his name was Deshaun. She was a single working mother and she had a hard time keeping Deshaun out of trouble where they had lived in the city, so she transferred to the small hospital in Angel Cross, where she worked as a nurse. She and Deshaun moved in with her parents until she could find a place for them to live. Josh hadn't met any of them, not until the incident at the park.

He hated the thought of having to tell his good friends about what their grandson had done. They were some of the nicest people Josh had ever met and he argued with himself whether or not he should do this to them. Then he felt a strong urging to tell them. He figured it was the Holy Spirit doing the urging. As he drove he rehearsed what he would say to them.

He parked his car on the curb in front of the little yellow house and walked up to the door. He rang the doorbell and waited. Soon the door opened, it was Jasmine. "Joshua, is that you? You're all grown up now!

Get yourself in here and give me a big hug! How's your mama?" She rattled on so fast that he didn't have time to respond. "What you doing over here? Are you here to see that old Riley? He sure would like to go fishing with you again! Did you know our daughter and grandson are living with us now? They came here last week, drove all the way from Chicago!" "That's great Jasmine, um, that's kind of why I'm here," he said nervously.

"Grandma, I, I have something to tell you," the boy said as he came slowly down the steps. Jasmine sensed that something was wrong. "I take it that you two have met?" she said looking at her grandson with suspicion. "Yes ma'am, we've met, I mean I don't know his name and he doesn't know mine, but we've met alright," Josh said. "Sit down, both of you and tell me what's going on," she said in a tone that no one would argue with. Deshaun told his grandmother everything and Josh was relieved that he did. Jasmine sat quietly and listened while shaking her head. Then she spoke slowly to Deshaun so he would hear every single word she said.

"This is what you are going to do young man," she said looking over her glasses at him, "you are going to pay for what you did to Joshua in any way he sees fit." Deshaun interrupted her, "I shouldn't have to do what he says! White men always get their way! We always have to struggle while they get everything they want! I'm tired of people like him telling us what to do!" he said angrily. Jasmine stood up and spoke slowly and thoughtfully, "I don't know who has influenced you to think that way Deshaun, but if you'll allow me to speak, I will tell you something that may change your mind. She sat back down in her rocking chair and spoke, "I once felt the way you do about white people. It filled me with hatred and anger each time one of them would talk down to me or order me around. Even some of the nice ones made me angry because I knew they were giving me special treatment. It felt like they were trying too hard to compensate for the mean white folks."

Josh sat quietly trying to hold his tongue. Deshaun sat on the edge of his seat, excited that his grandma related to him so well. "I know, what you mean! They think they are better than us!" he said. "When I became a Christian, the way I thought began to change and I began to see people differently," she said. "I hear you Jasmine! It's the same with me!" Josh interrupted. She smiled at him then continued, "Instead of seeing black people and white people, I saw lost people and saved people. All of us are sinful, no matter what color. We all need a savior. There are just as many black people who do wrong as there are white people. It's not the color of our skin that causes division and racism, it's our sinful nature. Only Jesus can change our attitude about others. Only he can give us a new nature. When he comes into your heart, he changes you and cleanses you from within. You become a new creation. I'm not the same Jasmine I used to be. I love others no matter what they look like," she said "I know what you mean, he changed me too!" Josh agreed. Jasmine walked over to Josh and took his hand. "You see Deshaun, Joshua is my brother in Christ. We are both God's children. You can be his child too," she said.

She changed the subject slightly. "Did you know that your great, great, great, great grandfather was the first minister of this town?" she asked. That surprised Josh and he just had to interrupt her, "Excuse me Jasmine, did your family get one of these crosses?" He pulled the wooden cross necklace out of his shirt to show her. "Oh my goodness, yes we have one too!" She went to her china cabinet and opened the drawer. She took out an old wooden box and opened it. "Here it is, right where I put it." She sat back down on her chair and held it out for them to see. "It was given to my great, great, great, maybe another great aunt Marvel. She was one of the little girls that got lost in the blizzard. An angel gave this to her, imagine that!" she said rocking back and forth in her rocking chair. "Grandma, do you really believe that?" Deshaun asked.

"It's true Deshaun, it really happened!" Josh said while suddenly feeling very forgiving toward the young man. Deshaun couldn't be over 13 or 14, he thought. "May I see it Jasmine?" he asked. She carefully handed it to him. He read the carved word, "FRIEND" on it. "It's from the Bible, "He is friend that sticks closer to us than a brother" she said. "What does yours say Joshua?" she asked. "It says, "GOOD SHEPHERD", I got this from an old man, or an angel, when I was a boy". They put away the crosses and returned to what they were originally talking about. "Well Joshua, what would you like Deshaun to do to pay for what he has done? Would you like to call the police?" she asked soberly. "No ma'am, I don't want that." He put his head down and thought about it. "I would like my grandfather's ring back. And, and, I've got it, I would like him to help me build a chest for someone. And I also would like him to help me fix a porch for an old lady that lives by me."

Jasmine smiled and looked at her grandson. "Where is the ring Deshaun?" "I called James, he said he dropped it in the woods somewhere, we'll never find it!" he said. Josh took a deep breath as he remembered what Jesus had said about forgiveness. "It's okay Deshaun, just help me with the other things and that will be enough." he said. "What do you have to say to that Deshaun?" Jasmine asked. He stood up and shook Josh's hand, "I'm sorry for what I did to you and your girlfriend, please forgive me," he asked.

Joshua stood up and said, "I forgive you. Don't get in trouble anymore, you've got a great family that loves you and cares about you and I'd like to be your friend if you let me?" he said. "Can you play catch with me sometime?" Deshaun asked. "Are you kidding, I'd love that! And maybe we can go fishing with your grandpa sometime!" he added. Deshaun seemed really excited about that idea. They went on and on while Jasmine rocked her chair and smiled. Then she said the words that she had heard her own mama say many times, "This gonna work jus fine Lord, this gonna work jus fine."

Josh left Jasmine's house and drove to the home improvement store to pick out some wood for his projects and then to the mall where he had already planned to meet Kayla. It wasn't a huge mall but it big enough for Angel Cross. While they sat in the food court, sipping on fruit smoothies, Josh told Kayla all about what had happened earlier and she was excited to meet Deshaun and talk to him. They walked around the mall, Kayla bought a couple of things from her favorite store, then went into the children's store to pick out some baby clothes and things to put in the chest Josh was going to build for Karly's new baby, Landon. They walked around the store holding up little outfits and toys, putting some into their basket.

They didn't know they were being watched. Josh hadn't met her, but a woman from his new church was also in the store. It only took two minutes for her to step outside and call her friend and tell her that Cami's son Joshua and his girlfriend were going to have a baby, and they weren't even married yet! "And I'm pretty sure Cami's husband has run off with another woman... yeah, I don't believe he's working either, two years, come on, no one believes that!" she said. The woman went on to discuss Bethany, "My sister said that she saw Cami's daughter.....um, Bethany, Brittany, I'm not sure? Right, yes, she saw her down by the lake smoking pot or something..... I know! The whole family's falling apart!" she said.

After they left the mall, Josh called home to ask if Kayla could come over for dinner, his mother was more than happy to have them stay home with her on a Friday night. She asked them to pick up a movie and some popcorn for later. She had spent a lot of week-ends home alone so she was excited about having a family night. *"Maybe they would like tacos"*, she thought, *"and ice cream for dessert!"* She quickly got dinner going, swept the floor, polished the furniture and vacuumed the living room. Then she ran upstairs to change her clothes. She really liked Kayla and she hoped that Josh would one day marry her. And although she hadn't known them long, Kayla felt very comfortable being around Josh's mom and sister it was like she was meant to be a part of his family.

Josh brought her in the back door where his mom and Bethany welcomed her with big hugs. They invited her into the kitchen where the food was set out in colorful dishes. Cami was gifted in the art of cooking and entertaining, she always made the table look so beautiful with special little touches. She made her family and guests feel special because she went through all the trouble to decorate. In the basement she kept storage bins for each party theme, and she loved having any excuse to decorate for a dinner party, the theme for the night was Mexican fiesta! Pastor Dan had even teased that she might be asked to decorate for the "Marriage Supper of the Lamb".

Everyone loved the decorations, Kayla and Josh danced to the festive music and they all enjoyed making their own tacos and ice cream sundaes. After dinner Josh suggested they play a word guessing game, he got the idea from Joe's family. He even got Bethany to join in and she actually had a lot of fun. Before they put in the movie, Josh started a fire in the fireplace while his mom passed out bowls of buttery popcorn and beverages. Everyone got comfortable, Bethany stretched out on the love seat, Cami called the recliner, Kayla and Josh sat on the floor and leaned against the broken sofa. It all felt so perfect, Josh loved this feeling, it was better than hooking a big fish or hitting a home run, it felt like there was nowhere else he would rather be. He looked around the room and thought this prayer:

"Thank you for my family Jesus. And thank you for Kayla. You have given me everything I need! I love how you watch over us and take care of us. Are you here? Why don't you join us, I want you here with me, in fact, I want you to be a part of everything in my life! And, oh yeah, thanks for sending your angels to guard us, it makes me feel really safe, knowing they are there."

"I watch over everything I've created, even the tiny sparrows! You are much more valuable to me than they are!" Jesus responded.

Meanwhile Josh's Guardian was up on the roof with two of his friends, Jade and Sapphire. He was entertaining them with some stories of his many adventures with Joshua, his current assignment. Gabe spoke fondly of Joshua and although he was an angel and Josh was a human, he loved him like a brother. "Joshua really keeps me busy! I've had to appear to him in human form twice already, and he's only 19!" he laughed. "Really, tell us about it!" Sapphire said as she got comfortable on the gable of the roof. "Well, the first time was when he was eight years old. His family and Kyle's family were camping in the woods north of here, near Big Bear River. He and Kyle wanted to go exploring in the woods, their parents told them to stay close to the camp. At first they did, but being adventurous, they wandered farther and farther away. The thrill of the exploration overrode the warnings of their parents!" Gabe shook his head and smiled as he remembered the scene vividly in his mind.

"They were climbing around on the hill with all the big boulders, fearlessly jumping from one huge rock to another. Kyle's foot slipped and he fell into one of the deep crevasses. The boys panicked when they realized that he couldn't climb out. Joshua tried to reach Kyle but his little arms weren't long enough or strong enough. He knew he had to find a grown up, and fast! Assuring Kyle that he would be right back with help he ran off to find their parents….in the wrong direction!" Gabe said, shaking his head again. "Did you give him signs that he could follow?" Jade asked. "Yes, but he was too scared to notice them. While he was running he tripped on a branch and cut his knee. He started to cry, more out of fear than pain, I think. I tried to comfort him, but he couldn't see or hear me, it was more than I could stand! I hated seeing him hurt and afraid like that, he was so little and helpless!" he said. "Oh, you're so sweet Gabe, you really love that boy, don't you?! Sapphire said. "Yes, I sure do!" he responded.

"What did you do then?" she asked as she sat up, signaling that she was deeply interested. "Well I figured he was going to keep running in the wrong direction so I asked for permission to appear to him in a human form. Permission was granted by the Lord personally!" Gabe said as he smiled and pointed toward Heaven. "He is so awesome isn't he?" Sapphire said, speaking of the Lord. "He is an awesome God! Speaking of awesome, there goes a warrior angel!" Gabe said pointing up to the night sky. They all turned to watch the streak of light. It was an angel of the Lord off on a mission, probably to do battle with one of the fallen angels. "I love watching the warriors! Look how fast he flies!" Jade said as he admired the angel's speed and agility. "Yes they are extraordinarily fast and strong, but I prefer being a guardian." Gabe said. "I agree, I love being a guardian too, there's nothing like it!" Jade said.

"Back to the story, tell us more!" Sapphire said, clapping her hands to get Gabe's attention. "I appeared to Joshua in the form of a harmless old man sitting on a rock, fishing in the river," he said. "What happened next?" the angels asked. "I saw Josh bend down to pick up a big stick, for protection I guess." he laughed. "His parents had warned him about strangers. He yelled hello from a distance then he asked me for directions back to the campground. I slowly walked over to him, held out my hand and told him not to be afraid. Seeing that his knee was bleeding, I asked him if I could bandage it for him and he agreed to let me.

While I wrapped the wound, I told him a story to calm him down." "What story did you tell him?" Jade asked. "I told him the story of the good shepherd. Then I reached into my pocket and pulled out a cross. I gave it to him and told him it was to remind him of the story." he said. "You gave Joshua one of your special carved necklaces?" Sapphire asked smiling from ear to ear. "Yeah, he got one!" he said, also sporting a huge smile.

"That boy has always been special to me! I loved him right from the beginning. He was the cutest baby ever and he was always doing the funniest things!" he laughed. "As I recall, you thought little Abigail was super cute too!" Jade added. Gabe got a thoughtful look on his face, "Yes, she was a little doll, wasn't she? Then again, so were Margaret and Molly, the Dutch twins that were born in 1794, they were so sweet and sooo adorable! And chubby little Maxim, can't forget about him! He was a real handful, hard to watch! Do you remember him Sapphire? He grew up to become a Roman soldier. One day he overheard the gospel from some prisoners he was transporting to Rome. The message touched his heart and turned his life over to Christ. He secretly met with the Christians and over time he grew strong in his new faith. He became a powerful witness to the other soldiers, until one of them reported him,"

Gabe said with a frown. "Oh yes, I remember him! He was a faithful and brave man, a true follower of the Lord!" she said. "Brave enough to face the lions in the Colosseum!" Gabe said proudly. "The Father instructed me to stand down that time." He pounded his chest and said, "He was a valiant warrior, a mighty man of God and he was…. he *is* my friend." Gabe had watched over many people through the ages and he cared deeply for each of them.

"Anyway, back to the story. I told Joshua to follow the river and he would see the campground just over the big hill," he said, pointing toward the hill in his story. "What happened to Kyle, where was his guardian?" Jade asked. "Timothy was with him. He tried to comfort him until help came," he replied. "How did he get him to calm down?" Sapphire asked. "It's funny how a little toad can make you forget all about your troubles!" he laughed. "What happened next?" Jade asked. "They found him alright, he was fine, a little scratched up, but fine." "Does Joshua still have the necklace?" Sapphire asked. "Yeah, he's actually wearing it right now!" he said with a grin, "he hasn't worn it in years! The Father sure knows the how to arrange things, it's no coincidence that Josh found it again. I'm sure a plan's coming together and I can't wait to find out what it is! It's true what they say, "God works in mysterious ways!" They all smiled at that.

Kayla sat next to Josh on the floor as they watched the movie. She looked over at him and saw a leather cord around his neck. "What this?" she asked as she pulled it out from his shirt. "Oh, that's my Angel Cross," he said smiling down at her. "It reminds me that the "Good Shepherd" is always looking out for me." Gabe smiled when he overheard Joshua say that.

The three angels decided to sit at the patio table on the deck before continuing their conversation. "So Gabe, tell us about the other time you appeared to Joshua," Jade said. He propped his head up with both hands, waiting anxiously to hear the story. "Yes, tell us what happened!" Sapphire said wanting to hear all about it. "Ryan and Brady are fast asleep, so I have time." She and Lance were guardians over the boys.

"Well, the second time I appeared to him was when he was sixteen," he said as he pictured it in his mind. "He had just gotten his driver's license and he was anxious to take the car for a drive on his own. He "borrowed" his brother's kayak and headed for the river. Oh, but Joshua being Joshua couldn't kayak in calm water, nooo, he had to go down the rapids! First, he went alone, which was a bad idea, and second, he had never been down those rapids before! It was about a half mile upriver where he put in. He did fine in the calmer water, but when he came around the second bend he was surprised to see a waterfall. It wasn't a real big waterfall but Josh wasn't experienced enough to handle it. He didn't have time to paddle away from it before the force of the rushing water pushed him over the edge! The falls held him under for a few terrifying seconds but he managed to right the kayak and paddle away from it only to get stuck in a swirling whirl pool!

He hit his head on a large boulder and capsized then watched helplessly as the kayak floated away toward the dangerous rapids while he clung to the rock for dear life. Holding on to the rock was very difficult for him because of the strong current and because it was late September, the water was freezing cold! I immediately took to the air, flying high above the cliffs to search the area. From there I could see for miles but I didn't find anyone close enough to get to him in time. I had to act quickly or he would die in the icy water. Again I asked permission to go to Joshua in person. God allowed it, and that time, he sent Timothy with me," he paused for effect. The other two angels nodded and smiled, acknowledging God's goodness.

"Tim and I rode in on four wheelers, dressed like park rangers," he said, standing up so he could act out the story more effectively. "We approached from the opposite side of the river because there was a sheer cliff on the other side, where Josh was. I tied a rope around my waist and dove in." Gabe was very demonstrative as he spoke, using his arms to make swimming motions. "When I reached him, he was shivering uncontrollably and his lips were turning blue. Timothy pulled us out using his ATV. Josh was dripping wet so Timothy wrapped him in blanket and quickly started a fire to warm him up." "Timothy sure makes a good boy scout!" Jade teased. Gabe nodded and said, "He does come in handy in an emergency! And, he just happened to have a thermos of hot chocolate with him, imagine that!" he laughed.

"The poor boy was still shivering so Timothy took off the jacket he was wearing and put it over Josh's shoulders. We sat with him until he dried off and warmed up. When he finally felt better we put out the fire and drove him to his car. He hugged us and thanked us one last time before we left. He went to open his car door and saw that he was still wearing Tim's jacket, he turned around to catch us, but we were already gone! His mouth fell open, he couldn't believe it! It had only been two seconds! We had vanished into mid-air!" he demonstrated Josh's expression of surprise. "I just love doing that! Makes them wonder," he laughed. "Josh still has that jacket. He tried to return it to the ranger's office but they had never seen one like it. They found the word "Guardian" on one of the emblems. And they'd never heard of two tall muscular rangers named Gabe and Timothy!" he said, flexing his arms to emphasize.

Kayla looked at Josh's face and noticed a small scar above his eyebrow. She lightly rubbed it and asked, "How'd you get this scar?" "Oh, I got that when I went over a waterfall in my kayak," he answered nonchalantly while feeling very proud that he had a cool scar to remember it by. To him it was a badge of honor, he had survived the rapids of Big Bear River...., with a little help from his *angelic* friends, that is.

20

The Word Hidden in his Heart

Kayla said goodnight and thanked Cami for the dinner and movie. As she and Josh walked to her car they made plans to see each other the next day, it seemed that they couldn't bear to be apart for more than that. He kissed her good night then watched as she drove away. He was slowly walking back to the house when his mother opened the door and waved him in. She was holding her cell phone to her ear and smiling, "It's Uncle Bobby!" she whispered while continuing to listen to what he was saying. "He'll be here tomorrow afternoon!" she relayed the message to Josh and Bethany who were hovering around her, waiting to hear more. She told Bobby that she would have lunch ready for him, all of his favorites, then she said goodbye and hung up the phone. "He said it again, he has good news about your dad!" she laughed. The three of them were so excited about seeing him that they huddled together and jumped up and down, squealing and laughing like they had won the lottery or something.

"We have to get this house clean!" she said with panic in her voice, "quick, stash this stuff in the closet!" she handed Bethany an armful of magazines and junk mail. "And you," she pointed at Josh, "grab those garbage bags, move, move, move!" she sounded just like a Marine drill sergeant. They all began to scurry around the house like a bunch of squirrels hiding nuts. After everything was back in order, they said good night and went to bed but they were too excited to sleep. Josh lay on his bed and tried to imagine what Uncle Bobby might tell them. Then he thought about how his sister had responded to the news. *"I'm glad that*

Bethany was excited. Maybe she's getting back her old self again." He was getting sleepy and his thoughts were starting to blur together. It was hard for him to have a clear thought at that point and before long he was sound asleep.

"Hey Josh, you've played hide and seek before, haven't you?" Jesus asked as he entered the room. Josh turned and was delighted to see his friend again. "Of course I have, why?" he asked. "I've hidden my word in your heart house and I want you to find it. When you find it, there will be a challenge for you. You will be rewarded if you pass the test," Jesus said. "Great, I like a challenge and I love rewards!" Josh said rubbing his hands together in anticipation. "Okay then, go find it!" Jesus yelled waving a checkered flag. Josh ran downstairs and looked in, on and around all of the furniture but couldn't find the bible anywhere. Next he raced upstairs and searched all around the living and dining rooms. He didn't find it there either. Then he ran up to search the bedrooms. He looked in all the closets and searched under all the beds and dressers, checking everywhere he could think of. He sat on the side of the bed and tried to think of anyplace he'd missed. "The kitchen, I forgot to look in there!" He raced down the stairs and slid across the tile floor. He opened every cabinet in the kitchen but couldn't find it. Tired and out of breath, he poured himself some iced tea and sat down to think. *"Where could it be?"* he wondered, *"I've looked everywhere in this house!"* Then he noticed something black on top of the fridge.

"There it is! It's always in the last place you look!" he laughed. He reached up and grabbed it. "I FOUND IT!" he yelled out. Suddenly a trap door opened up under his feet and he fell into the dark hole in the floor. It felt like a slippery waterside without the water. He slid down and around so fast that he could hardly catch his breath. It was the same feeling he got whenever he rode a roller coaster, it made him want to scream and laugh at the same time! Suddenly he shot out of the dark tube, flew through the air and landed in a pool of soft foam blocks. While struggling to get out he thought to himself, *"Wow that was fun.... and terrifying!"* When he finally managed to pull himself out of the pit, he stood to his feet he got a good look around.

He was in a large cavern like room that was lit up by the torches hanging on the walls. In front of him were two massive wooden doors. Out of the silence he heard a woman's voice softly say, "Choose one door Joshua, and open it." He glanced all around the cavern but didn't see anyone so he walked up to the doors and read the words that were engraved on them. The word on the left door simply said "BROAD" and the one on the right door said "NARROW". He scratched his head and searched the archives of his mind for any clues to what these words might mean. He thought to himself, *"I need to make the right choice. Who knows what I'll find behind these doors".* He remembered something, he couldn't remember when or where, but he knew he'd heard these words before, "Broad is the way that leads to destruction".

That settled it, he grabbed the handle to the door with the sign that said Narrow, opened it and walked through. He jumped a little when he felt a hand on his shoulder. He turned around and saw a beautiful woman in a flowing white gown standing before him. "Take this Joshua and follow the path," she said as she handed him a small leather pouch, then she vanished. Josh stood motionless for a few seconds with his mouth hanging wide open. He closed his mouth and looked inside the pouch. It was full of old coins. He pulled the strings tight and went to put it in his pocket but found that he was dressed like a Bible character, again. Looking around at his surroundings, he tried to figure out where he was. The place was hot and dry and there were rocky hills on both sides of the dusty path. He started walking down the narrow road then turned back to look at the door, it was gone! Assuring himself that Jesus wouldn't let him get lost or send him out to die in the wilderness, he kept walking. It was quiet and desolate out there, the only sounds he heard were the crunching of his sandals walking on the gravel and the screeching of the large birds circling overhead. As he walked along he wondered what his challenge would be. He soon got his answer.

He was startled when a man stepped out from behind a large boulder that was near the road. Then two other men jumped out, they were hiding behind some rocks on the other side of the road. Josh grew frightened when he saw the clubs that they held in their hands. He tightly clutched his bible in one hand and the money in the other, "Is this what you're after?" he said holding the bag out to them. They ran up to him and grabbed it then slapped the Bible out of his other hand. The biggest man hit him in the stomach so hard that it knocked the breath out of him. Then they all began beating him, so he fell to the ground and covered his head with his hands. He got to his feet and tried to fight back but the men overpowered him, clubbing and kicking him until he blacked out. Thinking that he must be dead, they ran off to count the money leaving him to bake in the blazing desert sun.

After a few minutes he woke up but he could hardly open his bruised and bloody eyes. He tried to get up but it hurt too much, he fell back to the ground writhing in pain. His lips were swollen and cracked from the heat and he had a horrible thirst for water. Trying to shade his eyes from the scorching sun with his hands, he heard something, it sounded like footsteps! He called out, "Who's there? Can you help me?" He squinted to see the figure of a man standing over him. "Help me, please!" he said in a dry, raspy voice. "Sorry, I, I have to meet someone soon, I don't have time," the man said as he hurried away. Josh rolled back and groaned. Not too long after that he heard someone else approaching. He mustered all of his strength and rolled over on his side to see who was coming. It appeared to be a priest wearing a long robe and a large hat. "Help, help me!" he managed to yell.

The priest stopped for a moment and looked Josh right in the eyes. Then he shook his head and walked quickly past him, never saying a word. "Come back, come back please!" Josh cried. The man kept walking. "THANKS FOR NOTHING, YOU JERK!" Josh yelled. Then his head dropped back down on the hard ground. Tears began to well up in his eyes as he prayed, "God, where are you, why is this happening? Don't you care?" Suddenly he heard footsteps running toward him. "I'll help you!" the man yelled as he quickly approached. Josh could hardly see the man who held his head up. "Here, drink this," the man said as he held a cup of cool water to his dry lips. He spat out a mouthful of bloody water then he drank down the rest. The man gently laid Josh's aching head back on a folded cloth and began to wipe the dirt and dried blood from his face. "Thank you, thank you for helping me!" Josh said, grateful to the stranger who had stopped to help him. Then his eyes slowly began to open and the pain began to fade away. "Feeling better?" the man asked. Josh slowly sat up and rubbed his eyes.

He turned to look at the man, "Jesus, it's you! Why... why did you let that happen to me?" he asked half mad because Jesus wasn't there to help him earlier and half overjoyed to see him now. "I never said life would be easy Josh, but I did promise to always be with you". Jesus walked over to the donkey and poured another cool drink from the jug hanging from the pack. He sat down next to Josh and watched as he drank it, then he asked, "What did you learn from this experience?" Josh stood up and checked himself for any damage. He thought about it and said, "Well, I hate what those guys did, I felt so helpless and outnumbered! It really made me mad! And I hate to admit it, but I was really afraid! But I think I'm even more mad at the two guys that wouldn't stop to help me, that really ticks me off! I never want to be like them!"

Then he started to remember the times when he done the same thing. Over the years he had seen plenty of people who had needed help, sometimes he'd stop to help but most of the time he didn't. It was easy to pretend that he didn't see the needs of others. He hung his head, ashamed to admit that he was just like them. "I'm sorry Jesus. I wish I could be more like you. You actually *do* care about people. I don't want to be that way anymore, can you help me change? Please, I can't do it without you!" he asked. Jesus reached into his pocket and pulled out a large gold coin. "Here, this is for you," he tossed it to Josh. Josh held it up and read the inscription "The Good Samaritan." Jesus put one hand on Josh's back. "Do unto others as you would have them do to you. Love your neighbor as much as you love yourself," he said as he patted Josh's chest with his other hand, "Hide these words in your heart so you'll always remember them, but don't just hear the Word of God, do it! Josh rubbed his sore jaw and said, "Your "Word" sure packs a punch! That was one painful story!" Jesus touched Josh's sore jaw and made the pain stop. "That feels much better, good as new, thanks!" he opened his mouth wide to check out his jaw bone.

"Oh, that reminds me, who was that woman back there in the cave?" Jesus smiled as he bent down, grabbed Josh's Bible and dusted it off. "That was Wisdom," he said as he opened the Bible to the book of Proverbs and handed it to him, "You can read about her right here," he pointed to the Bible then he winked at Josh and said, "If you're smart, you'll listen to her. Do not forsake Wisdom, and she will protect you; love her, and she will watch over you, that's in Proverbs by the way," he added.

In a blink of an eye he and Josh were wearing jeans, t-shirts and helmets. Josh started to say something, but his voice was drowned out by the loud noise of an engine. He turned around and saw Gabe as he tore around the curve in a four seated ATV. He pulled up next to Josh and Jesus and stopped in a cloud of dust. He yelled, "Hop in! I'm headed up the mountain. I'm going all the way to the stone cabin!" They got in and buckled up. When they weren't racing through the flat land they were bouncing their way up the rocky paths. "Where are we Gabe?" Josh asked through the headphone in his helmet. "We're in Arizona Josh, see the Saguaro cactus?" Gabe said pointing to the tall prickly plants. Stay with me now, we can go anywhere we want in your dreams! YEE HAW!" he shouted as they flew over a rocky ramp.

They drove through the beautiful but bumpy country for another ten miles before stopping to stretch. "Hoo-doggies, it's hot out here!" Josh said as he pulled off his helmet. "Yes, but it's a dry heat," Gabe replied as he tossed a cold bottle of water to Josh. "Step inside of that stone cabin to cool off," Jesus suggested, pointing to the old structure. Josh went inside and felt the temperature drop significantly. He poked his head out of the open window and yelled, "Hey, you were right, it is cool in here! Jesus, Gabe, where are you?" he walked outside and looked all around "JESUS, GABE, WHERE ARE YOU?" he yelled. "Not again!" he huffed. On the other side of the cabin there were some trees growing down in the dry creek bed along with some wickedly sharp cactus plants. He hiked down there and searched everywhere for them. "Why did you have to take the ATV?" he grumbled out loud to them, even though they weren't there.

He walked back toward the cabin and sat down on a large rock. "Now what am I supposed to do? Is this another test?" No answer came. As he gazed down the long dusty road he thought he saw a cowboy riding on a horse. He was approaching fast and stirring up a lot of dust. When he got close to the cabin, he pulled back on the reigns and brought the horse to stop. He wore a brown hat and a dusty poncho and he had a mean scowl on his whiskered face. *"He looks tough, but cool, like a gun slinger in an old western movie"*. Josh thought. The man turned his head to look at Josh and said, "I'm here for the gold." Josh didn't respond verbally he just shrugged his shoulders. The man pulled on the reigns and walked the big black horse toward him. His hand moved like a flash as he pulled out his pistol and pointed it at him. Josh jumped slightly then spoke to the gunman, "You know this is a dream, right?"

The man narrowed his eyes, shifted the cigar stub to the other side of his mouth and said, "Is it now, (spit), are you sure about that?" He cocked the gun and shot a big chunk out of the rock right next to where Josh was sitting. "I don't know anything about any gold mister!" cried Josh as he jumped to his feet and raised his arms. "I hear dying ain't much fun," the man said as he spit a gob of tobacco on Josh's shoe. *"That's disgusting! Now I am getting rid of these shoes!"* Josh thought. "What's that in your pocket?" the man asked. Josh reached into his pocket and pulled out the gold coin that Jesus had given him. "Ah, I can explain, um, would you believe God gave me this?" "You don't say. Well, the Lord giveth... and I taketh away," the man held out his hand. "But, but, this is my special coin, I earned this!" Josh said clutching the coin.

"The way I see it, you've got two choices, give me the coin...." he pointed the gun at Josh, "OR KEEP IT!" Someone shouted. They both turned toward the voice. It was Gabe! He was standing on a cliff above them. He was dressed in white cowboy clothes, and he held a shiny silver pistol with a pearl handle. With a loud "BANG", he shot the gun out of the man's hand.

Josh jumped and sat up in bed. It took a few seconds for his mind to clear. "It was a dream, thank God!" he said. It may have been a dream, but the noise was real. It was coming from downstairs. He got dressed and went to investigate. "Oh sorry honey, did I wake you?" his mother asked. She was hammering nails into the wall. "Do you like these pictures here?" she asked, "or would they look better over there?" she asked, pointing to the opposite wall.

"Why are you decorating the house this early?" he yawned. "I want it to look good when Bobby gets here," she explained. She was so excited about his visit and she wanted everything to be perfect for him. Normally she would be getting ready for church but under the circumstances she decided to stay home. She called the pastor's wife, Miriam to explain and ask for prayer. The time passed slowly for Josh, not so for his mother who busied herself with all the cooking and preparations, in fact, she wished for a little more time, fearing she wouldn't be ready in time. Josh was so anxious that he paced from the front room to the kitchen, looking out the window every few minutes.

At last, the meal was ready, the house was clean and everyone was waiting for the guest to arrive. A grey car pulled into the driveway. "He's here, get the door!" Cami said excitedly. A tall, thin man walked up to the door. "Bobby, is that you?" she asked. The last time they had seen him, he was a lot bigger around the middle. Bobby (Robert) was a nice looking single man who had been friends with the family for years. He and Derek were hired by the same company at the same time and they had been all over the world together because they did the same type of work. "Look at you, you're too thin!" she said as she looked him over. "I made a meal that will put some meat back on you!" she teased, "all your favorites, roast beef, potatoes and gravy, corn on the cob and homemade apple pie with ice cream!" "That sounds great! I'm so hungry I could eat a camel, but roast beef sounds a lot better!" They all laughed and hugged each other. Then Josh and Bethany led him to the dining room where they waited on him and made him feel right at home. They wanted to let him enjoy his meal before they asked, but he knew they were dying to hear about Derek.

"I know what you were told about Derek and me, but it's all a lie!" Everyone put down their forks and listened. "We weren't smuggling drugs......but we were smuggling," he said with a dramatic pause. They didn't interrupt but sat quietly anticipating what he would say next.

"Derek and I were helping a friend of ours sneak Christians out of Saudi Arabia, while secretly smuggling Bibles in!" Cami broke out in tears of pure joy, "I knew it! I knew you were innocent!" She smiled and hugged him. They all let out the breath that they had been holding in. "Tell us what happened? Where were you? How did they catch you? Were you in prison?" Josh asked, relieved that his dad had done a noble thing and not a criminal thing. "The Saudis caught on to us after about six months or so. We tried to be careful but maybe we got overly confident, I'm not sure? They arrested us, but not before we had helped **thirty eight** people to escape, most of them families!" he said proudly. "And I can't count how many boxes of Bibles we snuck in!" he added. Josh smiled wide and said, "That's so awesome Uncle Bobby!"

"They took us way out into the desert and kept us there in a small building. We had no way to communicate to anyone! It was tough out there, horrible food, horrible heat, bad water!" Bobby said, shaking his head. "How did you get away?" Bethany asked. "Well, that's what I call a real miracle!" he said excitedly. "I really can't explain, it was kind of like what Peter experienced in the Bible. One day all of the guards took off in their trucks. For some reason all of them left together! Then, this is the weird part of the story…, this big blonde guy busts in the front gate, he opens our cell door, easy as pie and helps us escape! Then Derek, me and our Jewish friend Avi hop in this guy's ATV and speed away!"

"Did you say a "big blond guy" in an ATV?" Josh asked breathlessly. "Yeah, this guy was huge, like seven or eight foot tall! Anyway, we escaped through the desert, not on the road. This guy seemed to know right where he was going!" Bobby laughed. "Did he give you his name?" Josh asked. "No, he just said that he knew what had happened to us and that he had orders to rescue us, he didn't talk much. Now, I personally believe, and you can call me nuts, but I believe that guy was an angel." Bobby said with a serious look on his face. Josh smiled and laughed, "I believe he was too!" They all laughed with joy at the story.

"Before we got to the Gulf of Aqaba and to the boat that he had waiting for us, the big guy took us on a very interesting side trip. We actually saw the *real* Mount Sinai, the mountain of God! I had seen a video of it, but now I've seen it for myself and it's so amazing! It's the only mountain around there that's black and charred on top! That's because the fire of God himself was on that mountain!" He went on to describe the rock alter of the golden calf and the big rock that God told Moses to hit with his staff. The rock was split open and there was evidence of the water that flowed from it. He also told them that he had seen thousands of footprints carved on the rocky ground marking the land that God had promised to the Israelites. "It was all fenced in by the Saudis to keep the world from knowing the truth. How we got in, I don't know? But it happened!" he said shrugging his shoulders.

After that we drove to the Red Sea. It had to be the place where Moses and the Israelites crossed over on dry ground. There was a small ship waiting for us, an exploration vessel. The crew let us watch the monitor as a remote camera took videos of the sea floor. We saw corral in the shape of chariot wheels! They were all over the place!" he said excitedly. Cami interrupted him, "That's really interesting Bobby. And I want to hear more about it, but, I need to know what happened to Derek! Why isn't he with you?" she asked impatiently, afraid to hear the answer.

"That's what I'm mostly here to tell you; he's alive, but he's sick…. he's really sick, some sort of infection they said." he said sadly. They all jumped to their feet, "Where is he?" they asked. "He's in Israel, in a hospital. A wealthy family of Messianic Jews bought my plane ticket home. The good news is, they will pay for all of you to fly back with me as soon as you can. I'm sorry I didn't come to you sooner. I had to check on my parents first and I didn't want to say anything to you over the phone. I don't know who might be listening to my calls. We may still be in danger, or so I've been told. I'll never go back to that prison cell, ever!" he stood up full of emotion. "It took a lot just to get my passport and I.D. back! I don't want them to find me! I'm a little paranoid, I know." he said, slightly blushing. They nodded, understanding his fear.

"Please forgive me for taking so long to tell you about Derek, I didn't mean to make you to worry! Before I left the hospital he made me promise to tell you that he's so sorry he wasn't here for you, and that he can't wait to see you again!" Tears filled Josh's eyes. He turned to see that his mom and sister were also crying. "So, when can you leave with me?" Bobby asked. "Right now, you order those tickets right now Bobby!" Cami demanded, pointing to the computer. He walked over to the desk then turned back toward them again, "I almost forgot, he told me to give this to you," he said as he pulled something out of his shirt pocket. It was a wooden cross necklace. "The angel.... I mean the big guy gave it to Derek." Josh gasped and grabbed the necklace from Bobby's hand. He smiled as he read out loud the words that were carved on it, "OUR FATHER"

TO BE CONTINUED................

CPSIA information can be obtained at www.ICGtesting.com
Printed in the USA
LVOW07s0806091214

417850LV00004B/266/P